OH!

2009
CHIN MUSIC PRESS, *PUBLISHERS*
SEATTLE

A MYSTERY OF MONO NO AWARE

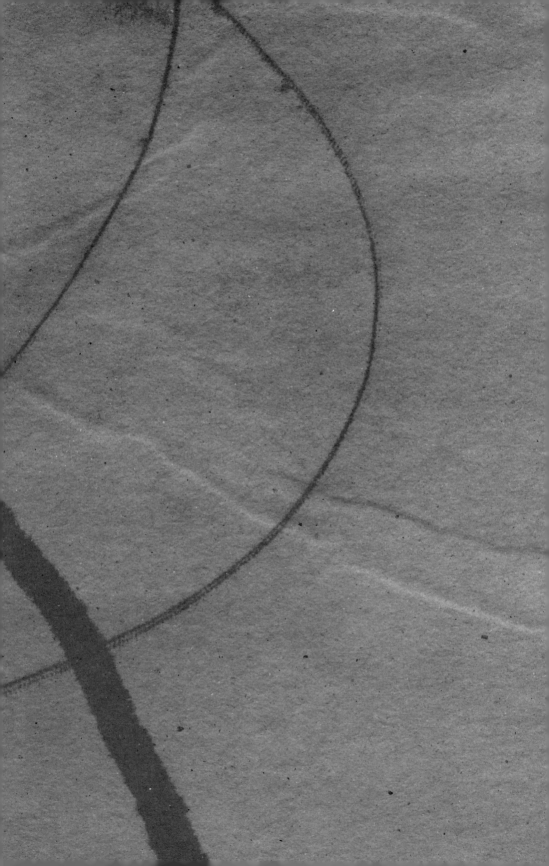

TODD SHIMODA

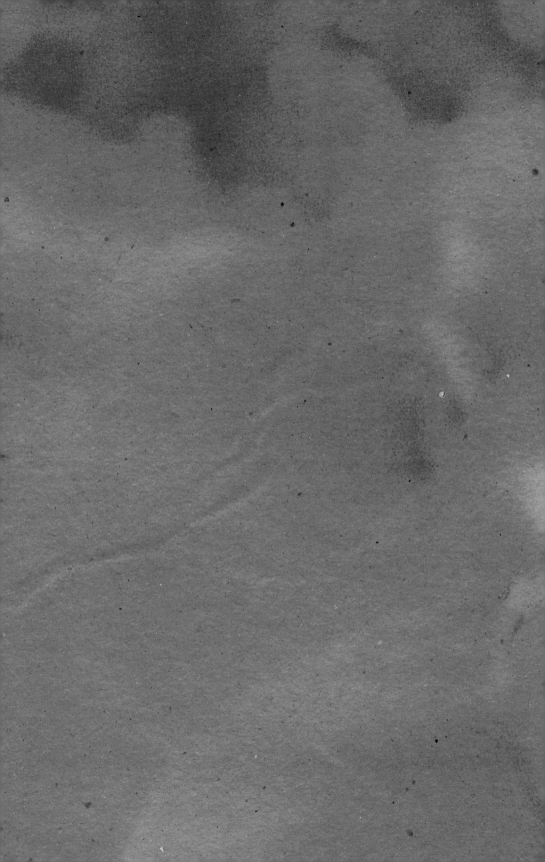

ART BY L.J.C. SHIMODA

mono no aware
("moh-noh noh ah-wah-ray")

mono - things, stuff
no - of
aware - emotion, especially a deep sadness

OH!

COPYRIGHT © 2009
by Todd *and* L.J.C. Shimoda

PUBLISHER:
Chin Music Press Inc.
2621 24th Ave W
Seattle, WA 98199
USA

http://chinmusicpress.com

First [1] edition

COVER ART: "SMALL THINGS" *by* L.J.C. Shimoda
BOOK DESIGN: Joshua Powell
Portions of Hokusai's "SOUTH WIND, CLEAR DAWN" and
"FUJI FROM A PINE MOUNTAIN" appear in this volume.

ALL RIGHTS RESERVED.

PRINTED in Thailand by the hospitable and capable folks at
Sirivatana Interprint Public Co. A special shout-out to
Mr. Meechai B. for putting up with our never-ending requests.
(Camera pans to CMP world headquarters. Large world map
entitled *"Better Know a Printer"* hangs over cigar-chomping boss's
desk. Iceland, the United States, Japan and now Thailand have a
CMP logo stamped on them. Anyone know a good color printer in
Turkmenistan?)

LIBRARY OF CONGRESS CATALOGING-IN-PUBLICATION DATA:
Oh! A mystery of *mono no aware*
by Shimoda, Todd

ART *by* LJC Shimoda; DESIGN *by* Joshua Powell; EDITING
and PROOFREADING *by* Chin Music Press

1. Japan — Fiction
2. Japanese culture — Fiction
2. Suicide — Fiction

ISBN 978-0974199566

ALSO BY THE AUTHOR AND ARTIST:
The Fourth Treasure
365 Views of Mt. Fuji
ALSO BY THE ARTIST:
Glyphix for Visual Journaling

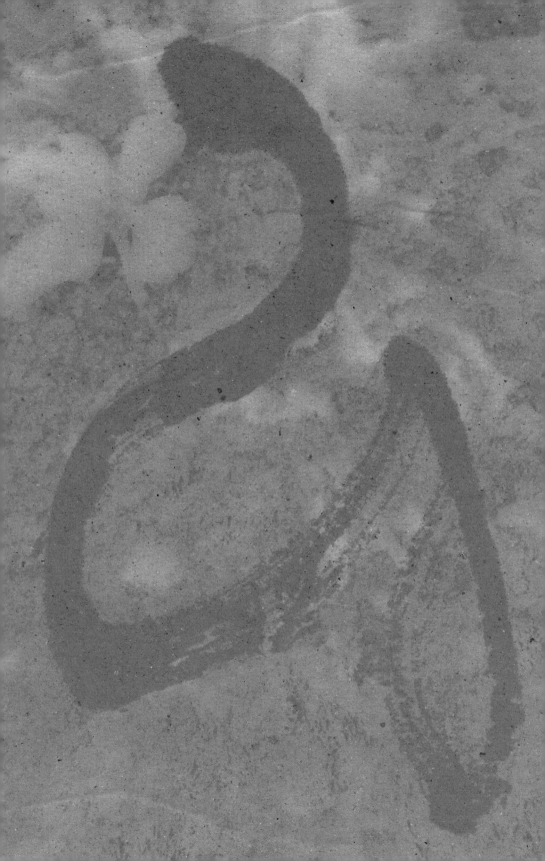

1.

I INHERITED A 1968 three-quarter ton Chevy pickup from my grandfather who mowed lawns and trimmed shrubbery in suburban Los Angeles until he was eighty-seven. He hired undocumented Mexican workers because his three sons and a daughter didn't want to mow lawns and trim shrubbery for a living. Very few people want to mow lawns and trim shrubbery for a living. When I was a teenager I worked for him one summer. After that I didn't want to mow lawns and trim shrubbery for a living. I never told him, but I'm sure he knew.

He got along well with the Mexicans perhaps because he made the effort to speak Spanish, perhaps because he paid them fairly. Maybe it was the lunches he provided, usually teriyaki chicken, black beans, rice, and an orange. I believe, though, it was because he could sympathize with them—he also started out in the U.S. of A as an illegal immigrant. When he was fourteen or fifteen or sixteen (depending on which of my uncles or aunt was telling the story), he stowed away on a Japanese ship carrying documented workers headed for South America. At a stop in Hawaii, he blended with the workers, claimed to have left his papers on the ship, and in the confusion slipped out of the port authority. Eventually catching a freighter, he ended up in L.A. when most of it was citrus orchards and oilfields. Preferring produce to petroleum, he worked in the orchards until they were plowed up and replanted with homes slathered in stucco.

Loading his mowers one morning, he dropped dead. No one knows what killed him, a stroke or a heart attack or whatever, because his three sons and daughter decided it wasn't worth doing an autopsy on the old man. It surprised the hell out of me when I heard he left me the Chevy. I'd never expressed interest in it although I always admired its raw power and how cherry he kept his beast of burden.

*

THE CHEVY RUMBLES LIKE a well-greased tank as it crawls in traffic on the 405. We reach my exit and I veer off the freeway. Three stoplights later, I find a parking spot, grab a cup of coffee and a breakfast burrito from Roberto's stall and hurry to my cubie in the glass-walled office building of Garza Engineering Services.

Joe Creed, another tech writer, pokes his head over the Garza-gray cubie wall that separates us, though not nearly enough. His flex schedule is offset a half-hour earlier from mine so he is always there when I arrive. He sniffs, says, "Hey Hara-san, not another breakfast burrito from Chez Roberto."

"Uh-huh," I mumble through a bite of tortilla, egg, potato, beans, and salsa.

Joe rests his arms on top of the cubie wall. "And that brownish liquid Roberto calls coffee …"

Joe brews his own coffee from a private stock of freshly roasted beans he brings to work. He acquires them from a mysterious dealer who takes only cash.

"Caffeine is caffeine," I say.

"Wrong, Burrito Boy. Coffee should be the gentle awakening of the palate with a superior bean brewed well." He spares me one of his lectures on roasting techniques, mouth feel, or aroma intensity and instead asks, "So, did you do anything last night?"

Joe mines my life for experiences. I'm sure he's writing a screenplay although he hasn't admitted it. Most of the tech writers at Garza are working on screenplays. The others are writing novels. Me? Neither. I like to read novels and watch movies, so why spoil them trying to write one?

I mean, does a novelist ever kick back and enjoy reading a novel? Not without comparing it to his or her work. Does a screenplay writer watch a film without thinking scene and plot points? I doubt it. Not to mention I did poorly in the creative writing course I took to satisfy a humanities credit. The professor claimed I lacked "emotional intelligence."

When I have time, I make up a story for Joe about stumbling on a drug deal gone bad or a tale about two sisters in a tattoo parlor. This morning I shake my head, turn on my computer, and raise my Styrofoam cup. Joe curls his lip and disappears behind the wall. I take another bite of burrito then open my latest project, a twelve-hundred-page opus in small font titled *Water Tower Design and Field Erection.*

*

"YOU'RE REALLY LEAVING?" Carine says. "For good?"

Carine is an Armenian name. It means "friend." Our relationship is like this: one-third lovers, one-third friends, one-third mutual counselors. We exist together yet not, in a benign parasitic relationship reaching the pinnacle of convenience. A 7-Eleven relationship.

"I'm really leaving," I tell her again. "I don't know about 'for good.' I'm not sure what that means."

"Let's examine this, Zack," Carine says. She pulls back a flip of her espresso-colored hair streaked with copper highlights and tucks it behind her ear. "Why now?"

"I don't feel anything."

"You don't feel anything." The psychoanalyst is in the building.

"Nothing. Except maybe frustration or annoyance now and then. But those aren't really emotions. They are reactions to irritation."

"Reactions to irritation," she parrots.

"I feel like I'm merely playing a role."

"What about pleasure? When we, you know …"

"Sure, that's pleasurable. Incredibly so. I'm not saying I don't experience moments of pleasure. It's that I feel empty of sustained emotion."

She waits a moment, probably thinking *How weird*, then says. "You don't feel anything except the occasional moment of frustration or pleasure."

"Nothing. No love, hate, sadness, happiness. It's chronic numbness."

"Really?" she says, now just Carine. "I've felt all of those today and it's not even like noon. I don't understand how you can't feel those emotions. How long has this been going on?"

I don't know. It wasn't like one morning I woke up and thought *What happened? You're an emotional eunuch.* There was a kind of slow awakening to the idea that I'm different than the average person on the street. "For a while," I say. "I'm almost thirty and can't imagine feeling, *not* feeling, like this for the rest of my life. I'm thinking a change of scenery might jar something loose. What do you think?"

"It might. Need a traveling companion?"

"Wouldn't work. And you know it. Besides, you've got the job you've always wanted."

Carine glances away and says nothing for a few moments. "I hope you find whatever it is you need."

"Thanks. I'll miss you."

Carine thinks about this too. "At least that's a start."

*

WITHIN A MONTH, I'VE quit Garza. To raise travel funds, I've sold most of my stuff, except the Chevy, which I leave with Carine who has a space in a garage she doesn't use. At my going-away party, she gives me a photo of the old truck. She promises to drive it once a week and check the fluid levels once a month. On the back of the photo she wrote: "I'll be waiting." I don't know if she means her or the truck.

Joe Creed shows up at the party wearing a leather jacket and smoking a Gauloises cigarette, its dark paper matching the color of his jacket. As a going away present, he hands me half of a pound of his precious coffee beans. He gets a little teary, either because of the pain of parting with the beans or because he's been assigned the task of completing *Water Tower Design and Field Erection.*

*

I DECIDE TO START my travels in Japan. I've never been there and it will be interesting to see the country where my grandfather was born. At the airport, I pick up a discarded *Los Angeles Times*. In the World section I read an article about three men and a woman who killed themselves at the foot of Mt. Fuji. They were found in a car parked in a forest named Aokigahara, apparently a well-known spot for suicide. The four met through a website for people wanting information about how to kill themselves. The news report translates the advertisement one of the victims posted on the website:

Applicants for suicide friends wanted. We will die of carbon monoxide poisoning. We can take sleeping pills and use portable barbe-cues to build up lethal gas in a car. I have everything ready. I will provide the pills and whatever else we need to anyone who wants to take part. Age/gender/reasons are no concern. The place will be Aokigahara. The plan will be carried out from September to October. Only serious applicants need apply. Let's face it, dying alone is lonely.

2.

WHEN SPRING ARRIVES IN Japan, Kumiko invites me to a traditional cherry blossom viewing party. She is one of the Japanese instructors at the English conversation school where I picked up a part-time gig after traveling around Japan for a couple of months checking out the scenery and brushing up my Japanese. I first learned a little of the language from my grandfather—counting to ten, names of plants, and some useful phrases like "Choke down the carburetor a little." When I needed a foreign language to satisfy a BA requirement, I studied Japanese all the way through advanced levels. After graduation, I surprised my grandfather with a conversation in his first language. He laughed at my formal diction and pronunciation. "Tokyo Japanese" he called it. As it turned out, he spoke a rough provincial dialect. Still I could tell he was impressed. None of his three sons and one daughter speak any Japanese, formal or not.

My teaching gig is undocumented as I don't have a proper work visa. I get paid under the table. Literally. The school owner slips me cash in an unmarked envelope under his desk. Ironic, isn't it?

So I accepted Kumiko's invitation, had to really, although I look on any planned event sponsored by our school with a lack of eagerness. Not because I'm antisocial; it's just that these gatherings are scripted to the minute. Our end-of-term party was an odd mix of games, stand-up comedy, and sing-along Beatles tunes, all choreographed by a professional host.

Kumiko meets me at the train station in Numazu, where I found my job and an apartment. Numazu, famous for its horse mackerel, is a smallish city on the Izu Peninsula, in the shadow of Mt. Fuji and on Suruga Bay. Kumiko is twenty-six and lived in Southern California for three years after college. She speaks fluent English with only a trace of an accent. She's dressed in a kimono for the occasion. It looks good on her although she shifts and adjusts it every few moments as we ride to Mishima, a town only a few minutes away.

"Do you have a girlfriend?" she asks me.

"Here or back home?"

"Either." She adds with a laugh, "Both?"

"Kind of one in LA."

"Kind of?"

Carine and I keep in touch with a weekly email, a monthly call. I guess she's still a girlfriend. "It's a long story. We're mostly just friends."

"No girlfriend here?"

I sigh and shake my head in an exaggerated show of disappointment. "How about you? Do you have a boyfriend here or there?"

"I had a boyfriend in LA, of course. But I was only staying for three years so I couldn't fall in love with him."

I wasn't sure I heard that right. *Couldn't* fall in love? "Why is that?"

"I wanted to go to California, it was my dream. My mother gave me the money to stay there for three years if I promised to come home after that."

"I mean how could you stop yourself from falling in love with your boyfriend? Don't you either fall in love or you don't?"

With a shrug she says, "You tell yourself not to fall in love."

"Could you also tell yourself *to* fall in love with someone?"

"I've never tried but I suppose you could."

We pass a small rice paddy. A man wrestles a power machine and two women bending at the waist push seedlings in the watery soil.

I ask Kumiko, "Have you ever been to the Aokigahara Forest?"

Concern crosses her face. "Why do you want to know about Aokigahara?"

"I've heard it's an interesting place."

"Every year like fifty or sixty people come from all over Japan to kill themselves in Aokigahara."

"Why there?"

Kumiko bites her lower lip. "There's a famous book, a mystery, about two lovers who committed suicide there. You don't want to go there. People get lost very easily. Many are found dead."

*

KUMIKO AND I GET out at Mishima Station and walk toward the large, old shrine named Mishima Taisha, the town's main attraction. At the shrine a row of fully blossomed cherry trees runs along the perimeter of the grounds. When I stop and stare at the eruption of soft white blossoms, Kumiko says, "Pretty." She tugs on my sleeve and we hurry away. Apparently, we aren't supposed to be looking at the blossoms yet.

A hundred or more people mill around the shrine. Those closest to the shrine ring clusters of clunky bells by pulling on thick, braided cords. After summoning the gods, the bell ringers clap their hands together three times, bow in silent prayer, then toss coins into the collection box. Kumiko finds an open spot and performs the ritual. I hang back until she finishes, then I step up to the bells and copy the ringing, praying, and tossing. My prayer is for an unstructured afternoon.

Kumiko leads me back across the grounds to the cherry trees where several knots of blossom viewers are claiming space. Mr. Kono, a middle manager whose hobbies are golf and playing violin (Conversational English Lesson 1: What is Your Hobby?), waves us over. He tells me that he arrived in the early morning to save our group a spot, delimited with a grass-green plastic tarp. When he was a junior employee, his boss sent him out to reserve a good spot for their flower-viewing parties. He was good at it, he let me know, although he believes in the Japanese saying: *hana yori dango*. He laughs after he translates: "I'd rather eat lunch than view flowers."

And eat lunch we do, from lacquered boxes neatly packed with raw fish, grilled fish, barbecued chicken, pickled vegetables, and rice sprinkled with black sesame seeds. We drink fizzy lemon soda, chilled sake, and cold beer. We sing songs and, to the titters of the rest of us, Mr. Kono and another student perform a traditional dance with symbolic hand movements that resembles a hula but without the aloha.

During the time we eat and entertain ourselves, no one comments on the cherry blossoms. No one even looks at them, at least not that I notice. Perhaps Mr. Kono's saying is true to a fault.

The cherry blossom viewing party lasts until dusk when, without a word of warning, everyone gets up and puts away the picnic supplies. Our departure seems timed, although I hadn't seen anyone look at a watch or heard anyone ask the time. We walk a few blocks to our "second party," a dinner at a local seafood restaurant where we eat crab and other shellfish and drink more beer and chilled sake. Exactly an hour and a half later, we get up and walk a block to our "third party" at a karaoke bar. I am coerced into singing an off-key version of "I Left My Heart in San Francisco." We sing and dance and drink for exactly an hour when we bow at each other, say good-bye, then disperse for the night.

A breeze picks up and swirls around Kumiko and me as we walk through the streets. She wobbles in her tightly wrapped kimono. I wobble too but from the combination of alcoholic beverages. We take a shortcut to the station through the grounds of the shrine. When we reach the middle of the cherry trees, the breeze becomes a wind.

A few of the delicate cherry blossoms float around us; I catch a couple of petals on my palm and show them to Kumiko. She smiles appreciatively, almost in wonder, as if it's the first time she's seen cherry blossoms. The wind gusts and the limbs of the cherry trees dance in fury. We are in a blizzard of pinkish-white blossoms. She looks at me wide-eyed through the fragrant snowflakes and cries out, "Wow!"

In only a few moments, the blossoms are torn from the trees and scattered across the grounds of the shrine. Kumiko grabs my hand and we walk to the station, stepping on blossoms already wilting.

3.

I GET A NEW STUDENT who signs up for private lessons. Professor Imai is a psychologist who studies the biology of personality. In his fifties, his hair is prematurely white but his face is boyish. He speaks impeccable English and takes lessons to keep it that way. Each week, he plans his own lesson by selecting a topic for us to discuss. His topics are usually in the vein of literary theory or aesthetics: structuralism, concepts of beauty, even hip-hop lyrics. I have to do a lot of homework to keep up with him.

His lesson is the last of the evening and our discussions spill over to his favorite bar. After a few whiskey-and-waters, which he insists I drink even though I'm not a whiskey drinker, when I'm slurring my words and rambling incoherently about West Coast versus East Coast rap, he maintains his precise English. He asks me to tell him my most memorable experience in Japan. I describe the cherry blossoms at Mishima Taisha.

He says, "Classic *mono no aware*."

"*Mono no aware*," I sound out the Japanese. "Let's see, I know that *mono* is 'things,' *no* means 'of.' *Aware* is a kind of sadness? Things of sadness?"

"It's difficult to define," the professor says. He savors a sip of his whiskey. "*Mono no aware* is about the hidden corners of things, the deeper meanings, not our superficial reactions to objects or events. A *mono no aware* event is not sentimental or symbolic but rather a true feeling that floats calmly throughout the mind and body. It's what we feel when we experience something that makes us cry 'oh!'"

"Oh," is all I can think of to say.

"Not that kind of 'oh,'" the professor says. "Oh!"

"Sorry. I have to admit I'm not fully understanding the idea."

The professor rubs his forehead. "It must be my English."

"No, no. Your English is perfectly fine, excellent. Beyond reproach. It's my feeble mind trying to grasp the concept. Maybe it's because I have trouble with emotions."

"Really? What kind of trouble?"

I wish I hadn't mentioned it. I've never talked with anyone about it except Carine and that was painful enough. "I'm not sure how to explain it, especially to a psychologist. It's like I don't have deep, sustained emotional experiences."

"Interesting. You haven't been diagnosed with autism, have you? Perhaps Asperger's Syndrome?"

"I've never talked to a professional about it."

"Can you understand what it might mean to experience such emotions, for example, when you watch a movie and see a character experiencing these emotions?"

"If you mean can I empathize, I suppose I can to a degree. I mean I can see that they are having some meaningful experience. But I couldn't tell you how it feels."

The professor gives me a long gaze then slips his hand into his shirt pocket and pulls out a business card. "Please come to my laboratory as soon as possible."

*

STANDING OUTSIDE THE DOOR of the professor's lab on the campus of Numazu University, I recall my high school biology teacher snipping the spinal cord of a living frog then opening its chest to show us its beating heart. I believe the procedure is called "pithing." I hope it's been banned.

I'm not sure why I'm here. When the professor invited me to his lab, sounding like a mad scientist in a low-budget horror flick, I answered "Sure" without a thought. Now I'm a little worried about getting involved in something like electroshock therapy. Or worse. Human pithing?

On the other hand, what do I have to lose? So far, traveling hasn't helped solve my problem. Sure, it's been a good time for the most part. Nice scenery, nice people. Certainly a lot of drinking. But nothing deeply affecting.

I walk into the lab and I'm hit with the medicinal odor of formaldehyde. Safety posters on eye protection and handling chemicals hang on the walls. Plastic, take-apart models of the human brain are arranged on the lab tables. The professor greets me and ushers me to one corner of the lab where a human brain rests in a shallow, clear plastic vat of preservative fluid. The brain looks unreal, not too different from the plastic models.

The professor says, "Our emotional experiences are troublesome from a scientific point of view. We know emotions can be moderators and agitators. We know about the complicated pathways that connect the sensory organs such as the eyes and ears to brain neurons that respond to the stimuli. Fear, for example, goes one way, pleasure another. And yet we lack a fundamental explanation of how this process causes pleasure to feel *good* or pain to feel *bad*. Even more problematic are the deep, complex emotions such as love or hate."

We put on latex gloves. Dipping his hands into the vat, the professor removes the brain and places it on a tray. He gestures for me to pick it up. I do so gingerly, expecting it to squish out of my hands like pudding. Instead it's raw cauliflower.

The professor says, "Such a small mass, only fifteen hundred grams, holds infinite thoughts and dreams. Creates symphonies and poetry. Imagines other worlds. But most mysteriously, it *feels*."

*

THE PROFESSOR DOES WIRE me up, but tells me it won't harm me in any way. On my head he places a device that looks like a swimmer's racing cap with wires running from it. He tapes some more measuring devices to my arms. After several minutes of adjustments, he asks me to silently read short poems as they display on a monitor.

31

In Springtime the blooming flowers
of cherries burst forth, but that alone.
In autumn the sadness of beauty
is really shown.

Is it only I who hears the loneliness
of crickets chirping
beside the wild pinks
in these evening shadows?

Spring brings plaintive mourning
even above the clouds,
and the sky is dark
with an ink-black haze of sorrow.

After a few other tests, we are finished and I ask him, "Did you find my problem?"

"Eh? No, you don't have a problem. These tests are just baseline readings. What did you feel when you read the poems?"

"I could visualize the images they describe, but I didn't feel anything."

"Good." He waves away the statement. "Not good for you, good for my research."

"Did you write the poems?"

"No. They are very old. Now," he says, "the next step is for you to get lost."

"Get lost?"

He looks dismayed. "That's not proper English? I mean you must go to a place where you have never been before and not know how to return."

"I see what you mean. Okay, I'll get lost. Then what?"

"At this point, don't worry about anything other than getting lost."

*

MY NEXT DAY OFF, I catch a bus then walk to the Aokigahara Forest near Mt. Fuji where the four young Japanese killed themselves. I walk along the road wondering where I should start the professor's vague and unexplained task of getting lost. It seems like a strange thing to do, but harmless. I'm sure I'll be able to find my way out even if I do get lost.

At the turnoff to a side road, I come across a piece of faded yellow police tape dangling from a sapling. A few steps away, I see a sign nailed to a tree. It reads: "Please reconsider your decision to die. Turn yourself into the police." Underneath the exhortation is: "Takegawa Citizens Group for the Prevention of Suicide."

As good a place as any to get lost, I decide. I walk on the side road for a while, then plunge into the forest. Walking is difficult over the rough field of lava. The trees grow in dense groves. Their knobby roots contort over and sometimes through the porous rock. As I go deeper into the forest, it becomes more impenetrable, the air dank and misty.

After about an hour, I sit on the moss-covered trunk of a fallen tree. The canopy of trees diffuses the sunlight and when a cloud passes over, the forest darkens. The mist rises and thickens until I'm swimming through a giant kelp bed at the bottom of the sea. If the trees released their grip on the rocky soil, they would float up to the sky.

I think of the four suicide victims who sealed the car windows and doors with tape, took sleeping pills, lit two grills, one on the front seat, one on the back. They must have been in ultimate despair. Is it better to feel nothing or feel their pain? I stand up and look around the forest.

I'm lost.

Mono no aware is difficult to translate literally, although the word "sensibility" is perhaps the closest single word. Sensibility is the awareness of and responsiveness toward something, as emotion in another. It implies a refined sensitivity to emotion and responsiveness toward the sorrowful. Other definitions of *mono no aware* include:

- traditional Japanese acceptance of the inherent sadness of life
- feelings generated by ephemeral beauty
- the enveloping sensation of refinement and grace in which the feeling and the mind come together
- sensitivity to things and events
- an aesthetic awareness of the transience of all things
- a feeling of being connected to nature and all things
- a desolate poignancy
- the intangibility or evanescence of objects
- a feeling for the poignant beauty of things
- wistfulness

4.

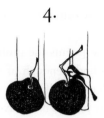

ANOTHER EXPOSED ROOT CATCHES the toe of my shoe for the hundredth time, but I don't fall. I've learned to walk with flexed knees and arms hovering like wings to keep from adding to my collection of bruises and slaps of dirt on my jeans. More than a few times I managed to just catch my balance with a fingertip grab of a low tree limb or rock.

At the initial moment of knowing I was lost, I felt, well, satisfied. I accomplished my task. But elation isn't the typical emotion lost people feel. They would be scared, worried, frustrated, fearful for their lives. So the professor's experiment has a fatal flaw—his experiment is confounded with the task. In other words, I set out to get lost, which is not a valid experience.

The elation is over and I'm experiencing the disorientation of being in a dark, treacherous forest. To top it off, I'm starting to drip sweat from the exertion. The wind died long ago and the dank humidity rose immediately, enveloping me like the embrace of an obese aunt.

Still I'm not really concerned. Being lost in my case means stumbling around the forest for a few hours at the most. Sooner, not later, I'm going to run across the road that the bus took to the small town where I started my trek. Keep going long enough and I'll walk right into the sea.

On cue, the slope levels out and the thick forest gives way to a pocket-sized meadow with a stream trickling into a pond. I sit on a rock and splash the cold clear water onto my face and rub it around my neck. For the first time since I got lost, I realize I'm parched. Of course, I hadn't brought water or food with me. Knowing me, if I'd thought about it, which I hadn't, I would have assumed that would be cheating on my task. I resist the urge to drink the stream water even though it looks clean.

The break feels good and I splash my face once more as the mosquitoes discover me. I take off, dodge the swampy spots along the periphery of the meadow, and follow the stream. The gurgling and splashing water is a pleasant companion.

I sound like one of those poems the professor made me read. Maybe that's what he wants me to find—enough of an appreciation of nature to write a poem, like: "A traveler lost, talks to his companion, a gurgling brook full of *aware…*" I pick up my pace as if to leave the poetry attempt behind.

*

THINKING BACK ON MY life, something I rarely do, I recall one of the strongest moments when I realized I was emotionally deficient—when I heard my grandfather died. I was kind of close to him in a way, close in the sense that I felt comfortable around him. He didn't say much, but was always pulling off a grin when it was needed. He didn't pat me on the head or ask how I was doing in school. But you could tell he was okay with me just being me. And when you're a kid, heck even as an adult, that's great.

Along the side of his and my grandmother's house was a strip of utility easement they'd reclaimed and made into a vegetable garden. And at one end my grandfather added a horseshoe pit. He wasn't a big guy, maybe five-feet, but he could really toss a mean horseshoe. Really got his whole body into it. When he'd get a ringer, a big grin would break out on his face and he'd shake his head apologetically. Like it was pure luck.

When I heard he'd died, that's all I thought of—him tossing a horseshoe.

*

FOLLOWING THE MEANDERING STREAM is easier than trudging through the forest proper. I'm finally getting irritated with being lost. I don't consider that an emotion, not a deeply felt one, if that's what the professor is hoping for.

Suddenly I step onto a road.

It's more a dirt path barely wide enough for a compact car. I look up and down, actually left and right if you want to be technical about it. I don't see a preferred way to go, no clue as to the direction closest to civilization. I think about flipping a coin to decide, but then turn right.

In a few minutes I come to a makeshift shrine just off the side of the road—a trio of bamboo stakes hammered into the ground, entwined with a sagging stretch of manila rope joining them together loosely but clearly implying a relationship. At the base of the bamboo stakes are a couple of shriveled, blackened oranges, a single-serving sake bottle, and a pack of cigarettes, its label faded to a blur of yellow-white.

Somebody, maybe three people, likely died here. The shrine reminds me of makeshift memorials where someone died in a car wreck, although this is not a likely spot for a traffic accident. Maybe a hiker got lost and died of exposure. Most probably, the shrine marks one of the forest's suicides.

Moving on, I soon come to a narrow valley cleared of trees and terraced with rice fields. Trudging toward me is a short, elderly man wearing rubber boots that climb up to his knees. His pants stick into the boots, billowing out from the tops like bloomers. He carries a shovel over his shoulder like an infantryman's rifle. Except for his militaristic posture, he reminds me of my grandfather.

The old farmer doesn't appear to notice me until I'm two steps in front of him. He jerks to a step, his shovel falling forward. I lean back in case he doesn't stop it from falling onto my head. He catches it in time and mumbles something I don't understand.

"Excuse me, grandfather," I try in my formal Japanese, "is there a bus stop near here?"

He gives me a suspicious look. I guess I do look suspicious coming out of a forest in the middle of nowhere looking for a bus. Then the farmer cackles, probably at my formal Japanese. He speaks more clearly this time, the gist being: "Bus? What are you crazy? Does it look like a bus is going to coming down this farm path?"

I laugh with him at my stupid question. I slap my forehead and call myself a fool.

When we finish making fun of me, I ask, "How about a town? Is there one this way?" I point the direction he came from and the one where I'm going.

"If you can call it that. More like a village."

"How about a bus stop there?"

"Of course there's a bus stop. What do you think this is, the sticks?"

I can see I'm always going to be challenged by his superior intellect. "Well then, gramps, how far is it?"

He gives me a nasty squint when I lapse into informal diction. He turns stiffly and looks back. After several seconds he turns back and shrugs. "Don't get there often myself. Probably for a long-legged kid like you, a twenty-minute walk."

"Thanks."

I start to leave him to his farming when he jams the shovel blade down in front of my foot and says, "What were you doing up here anyway?"

"Me? Just hiking."

"Hiking, eh? This is no place for hiking. Hey, you don't have a backpack or nothing. Not even a camera. No one goes hiking without a camera."

"I thought I was going only for a few minutes but got lost."

He slowly drags his shovel back to his side. "You don't want to get lost around here. You could get into a lot of trouble. We don't want people like you coming around here."

"What kind of person is that?"

Without answering he shoulders his farming implement and marches past me like a guard at a wartime checkpoint.

The kanji for *aware* is derived from the characters for "mouth" or "say" and "clothing." The latter is used for its pronunciation of the sound of lament, which humans make when experiencing deeply felt sorrow: Ai. This sound is nearly universal, an expression that all cultures would recognize, just as laughter is so recognized.

Considering all of these definitions together, *mono no aware* is an attempt to capture the harmony between the heart (or more precisely, the emotional mind) and objects and events. It can be found in the brightness of a spring morning as well as in the early autumn twilight; it is mainly composed of a nostalgic sentiment and a tender quietness. In extension, *mono no aware* may more precisely be a collection of concepts that explains how the Japanese view this aesthetic world. Among these many concepts are *mujô* ("bittersweet impermanence"), *wabi sabi* ("rustic beauty"), *yûgen* ("mysterious beauty"), and *miyabi* ("refined elegance").

5.

MY APARTMENT IS ON the top floor of a three-story building backing onto an alley that runs along the grounds of a rice packing plant. At sunrise, six days a week, the plant powers up with a hum and clatter. The noise used to wake me up but now I rarely notice it.

The building's owner, my boss's brother-in-law, gives me a break on the rent. So he says. The bottom floor is a yakitori restaurant. The grill's exhaust fan blows vaporized protein and fat into the alley and up into my window. The smell used to bother me but now I find it comforting.

On the second floor is a second-class bar. In other words, it's not a top tier place with elegant hostesses and twenty-five-year-old scotch, nor a dive serving diluted whiskey or cheap sake. The bar has a karaoke machine that fires up about ten most nights. The singing used to bother me. Now it bothers me a lot.

On the third floor are three apartments. I know the other two units are occupied although I've never met the residents. On occasion I'll hear a door open or close, hear the drone of a television. For whatever reason, we never cross paths. The apartments are tiny places yet fully contained with a kitchenette, a prefab bathroom unit, and just enough floor space to roll out a futon. A fearless, indestructible family of cockroaches has run of the kitchen. I've surrendered it to them and I only keep a couple of things in the mini-fridge. Luckily, it's pretty cheap to eat out in Numazu. Drinking out is not, so most of the contents of my fridge are of the liquid, alcoholic variety.

Other than a group of housewives that meets Wednesday mornings, all my classes are in the late afternoon and evening. After class, I hang out with students or Kumiko until after midnight when the last train leaves and at least until the karaoke machine in the second floor bar shuts down and I can come home to quiet. I stay up reading or watching TV until two or three. So I've gotten used to sleeping late, which works out fine since I've never been a morning person.

This morning Kumiko is sleeping with me, pushed up next to me, our skin slightly damp with perspiration. I got up at dawn as the rice packing plant was powering up to turn off the air conditioner because it was chilly. Now in the mid-morning it's getting warm on the single-sized futon.

Kumiko doesn't spend every night with me, less often than once a week. She has her own apartment and works two jobs to pay for it and other living expenses. We rarely have a morning off together.

She must sense I'm awake—she stretches and twists to the side. She blinks, sees me, says, "What?"

"Nothing."

"Time to go to work?"

"Nope. Not for a few hours. I feel like going for a run."

"That's crazy." She pulls the sheet off us and reaches for me.

*

WE'RE LOUNGING ON THE futon drinking cold green tea I bought from a vending machine on the corner. A daytime drama plays out its soapy plot on the television. That and the hum of my *aircon* drowns out most of the rice packing plant.

"Have you ever been lost?" I ask her in English. We alternate our conversational language between Japanese and English. Some things are easier to talk about in one language than the other. Talking about getting lost seems easier in English for some reason.

"I got lost in L.A. all the time. It's so big and you can't walk anywhere. I got lost a lot when I drove. For some reason I never get lost in Tokyo."

"What did you feel when you knew you were lost?"

"Um ... I don't know. Maybe a little scared."

44

"When you were lost did you feel something about yourself?"

Kumiko wraps her arms around her knees and lightly rubs her calf. I think of Carine who wraps her arms around her legs like that. Kumiko's long hair, colored to a stylish burnished mahogany, drapes loosely across her arms allowing a peek of her skin. "What do you mean?"

"I think if you are lost, you must feel vulnerable. Open to attack from strangers or from nature because you don't know what to expect."

She nods. "And the opposite is true. If you are in a familiar environment you feel safe. You know what is going to happen next, the kind of people you might encounter."

"Exactly. So which of the two situations do you feel you truly understand your being? I mean if you are lost you must feel the boundaries of yourself tightening in. You feel your skin. You feel your heart beat."

Kumiko traces her fingertips over her skin. "And when you are not lost, you expand? You feel larger, a part of the surroundings?"

"I don't know. Is that how you feel?"

"I suppose," she says.

*

WE SOAK IN THE bathtub together. It's a tight fit. But hey, that's good. "What do you want to do with your life?" I ask Kumiko.

"My mother has a traditional plan for me. Marriage, kids. That's why she wanted me to come back to Japan. She's old-fashioned. Most parents of women my age don't care about such things. 'Get a good job,' they say, if they say anything at all."

"What about your father?"

"He's old-fashioned too. In other words, he does everything my mother tells him to."

"But you don't want the traditional plan?"

She shakes her head. "I studied English and literature in college. I'd like to do something in publishing, maybe translating."

"Why don't you do that?"

"I've started looking. So you don't have to worry."

I'm not sure what that means. Before I can ask her to explain, she turns on the tap and gives us a blast of hot water for a few seconds. Then she turns and nestles her back into the curve of my front. With a little sigh, she guides one of my hands down to play between her legs and the other to caress her breasts.

I have a sudden thought that she and her L.A. boyfriend used to do this.

*

As we get dressed, I ask her about *mono no aware.*

"Huh?" she says.

I repeat the term, adding, "In English it's translated as the 'emotive essence of things.'"

"Where did you hear that?" she asks.

"From one of my students. Professor Imai. It's not a real literary term?"

"Oh it is. A real old one. No one except classics and poetry scholars use the term."

"So modern Japanese people don't really know about it? They don't feel the deep sadness or joy in things?"

"The term is from like hundreds of years ago and referred to poetry and novels written hundreds of years before that." She laughs and shakes her head. "No one has time for *mono no aware* anymore."

In many ways, *mono no aware* embodies the essence of human nature—how we think and feel, as well as how we express those thoughts and feelings, particularly through the arts.

While the concept is an old one, and one that is not in common use today, it provides an enlightening way to view the world and how to live in it. Efforts to understand the concept also represent a journey of discovery that follows paths of literature, art, and science, as well as those traveled in the physical sense. Many others have gone down these paths, and like rivers in Zen *koan*, they are the same yet always different.

Cherry blossoms are the prototypical *mono no aware* objects. They are tragically beautiful, blooming after winter's doldrums, trumpeting life for only a few days before they are gone. Seeing a cherry tree fully bloomed, it's hard not to stop and gaze at it, and say or at least think, "Oh! That's beautiful." But is it the cherry tree itself that is intrinsically beautiful or what we make of it? That question and others must be answered in finding the deep meaning of *mono no aware*.

6.

PROFESSOR IMAI'S DISCUSSION TOPIC this evening is the role of science, specifically cognitive science, in creating a difference between reality and the perceived world. You could write a book about such a complex subject—philosophers and scientists *have* written books on the subject—so it's a tough slog to get in anything meaningful in fifty minutes. I let him do most of the talking as I hadn't researched the topic except for a quick scan of some online philosophy of science articles.

Luckily, the professor suggests we end the lesson early and adjourn to his favorite bar. We walk a short distance from the school to a block of bars and restaurants paralleling the train tracks. The bar we enter is on the second floor of a narrow building. I've been there a couple of times with him. The bar doesn't have a name, at least not that I've heard or seen. There's only a simple neon sign saying "open." Inside, it's a cozy place of light wood and paper screens, filled but not crowded with five tables and five stools at the bar. The tables are occupied with middle-aged men well into their evening. The professor and I sit on a couple of the stools.

The bar owner, Mama-san (as the professor introduces her) greets us enthusiastically and politely asks if we are healthy. The professor points at me and says, "He is young and healthy," then points to his nose and says, "I am old and unhealthy."

Mama-san nods toward me. She's attractive, probably in her late fifties, and wears a kimono very well. "If one of you is going to be my lover then it's the young and healthy one."

The professor claps me on the shoulder. "Congratulations! I hear she's quite a tigress in bed."

"She'll eat me up?" I say and that brings howls of laughter.

When they recover, she takes our order. The professor insists we have whiskey from his own special bottle kept behind the counter. After Mama-san fixes our drinks, the professor asks me if I got lost yet.

"Yes. I took a bus to a small town I've never been to before. I went for a walk in the forest outside the town. After an hour or so I was lost. It took me a couple of hours to get unlost."

The professor's brow wrinkles. "Unlost? Is that a word?"

I grin sheepishly. "No."

"'Found' is the word? You got found? No, you can't find yourself if you are lost."

"Not in that sense." I start to explain what "finding yourself" means but he interrupts me with a wave.

"Right, right. I know the meaning of that idiom. So after two hours you found your way out of the forest."

Who's the English teacher here? "Right."

Mama-san serves us a few tiny plates of food. We take a sip of our whiskey—it's smoother than usual or maybe I'm getting used to it—and try a sample of the food. It's all delicious. Mama-san smiles when I tell her.

I ask the professor, "Do you want to know what I was feeling when I was lost?"

The professor inspects a bit of pickled vegetable between his chopsticks. He pops it in his mouth, apparently satisfied with the morsel. "If you want to tell me," he says.

Sounds like something therapist Carine would say. "I thought that was the object of the task, to get in touch with my feelings."

The professor shakes his head. "I had no preconceived results in mind."

For some reason I'm disappointed.

"But if you had some feelings," he goes on, "please tell me."

I tell him that I didn't think I felt the same as a person lost would actually feel.

"Oh?"

"People don't set out to get lost, do they? Getting lost was my goal and so I was happy to accomplish my task. People who get lost set out to go somewhere and fail to reach their goal. So they are frustrated and angry, maybe even scared."

The professor nods vigorously. "Exactly as you say."

"But…" I shake my head and take a gulp of the whiskey.

The professor says nothing. I chomp on crunchy pickled octopus.

Then I get it. "So it's the same with emotions. Purposely setting out to feel something, to experience an emotion, will never be the same as naturally experiencing the emotion. Right?"

The professor gives a little nod, then motions for Mama-san to refill our drinks.

*

WE'RE STILL IN THE bar after a couple of hours. We talked about science, my stellar technical writing career, and the definition of post-modernism. Then I steer us back to getting lost. "That's what the task was all about. And that's why you wanted to talk about cognitive science in the lesson tonight. You want me to know that science won't be able to help me with my stunted emotions."

"I wanted you to get something out of the experience. But there was no predetermined outcome. But you got something out of the experience. That's all that's important. It's the same with the lesson topic tonight. I had no motive in mind other than it is an interesting topic to me."

"But in my experience of getting lost did I achieve *mono no aware*?"

He sucks in a breath. "Difficult to say. *Mono no aware* is a sudden, intensely personal awareness."

"That definition is different from the one we discussed before, isn't it? I thought *mono no aware* is about the emotive essence of things. Now it sounds more like enlightenment."

"I'm sorry if I confuse you. There are several dimensions to the concept. One is the thing itself, its fundamental essence. The other is a person's reaction to it. Does that make sense?"

I rub my forehead. I'm a little woozy from the whiskey. Mama-san notices and says something to the professor I don't catch. Must be something to do with my feeble mental capabilities or my lightweight drinking ability. "You know," I say to the professor, "I asked someone else about *mono no aware* and she said no one in Japan today knows the concept. It's a really old term used only by a few scholars. She claims everyone is too busy to feel *mono no aware*."

The professor nods. "That's mostly true. The term can be a rather technical term in literary theory circles. And it is an old term, first used by Motoori Norinaga in the 1700s. Norinaga was part of the Japanese national arts movement, developing a theory to describe the development of Japanese poetry and fiction. He was a poet, essayist, traveler, and a doctor in the Chinese tradition."

"Motoori Norinaga?" I say when he pauses.

"Yes. Your friend is correct in saying not many Japanese use or understand the term. Probably not many people have heard the term. But I disagree that we are too busy to feel *mono no aware*. There exists a fundamental nature to Japan and the Japanese to experience *mono no aware*."

"You are saying it's intrinsic to the environment and the people of Japan. In other words, what Norinaga categorized as *mono no aware* was already there and it became expressed in the classical literature of Japan."

The professor tilts his head, thinks for a moment. "Yes, I believe that is the case."

"Does that mean other countries and peoples don't experience *mono no aware*?"

The professor folds his arms across his chest. "A difficult question to answer. I think in one sense I would answer 'no.' In every culture, in every environment there is a capacity for *mono no aware*. In another sense, yes. In Japan, through our unique culture, traditions and arts, even in our industry, there is a unique reaction to situations that I would call *mono no aware*."

"That's why you say *mono no aware* is still being experienced even though few people understand the term."

"Yes," he answers with a heave of air from his chest.

*

BEFORE WE LEAVE, HE gives me my next two tasks. The first is to find a pear-shaped rock. The second is to commit a petty crime.

EXHIBIT W015

In his work, Motoori Norinaga (1730-1801)
especially referred to *The Tale of Genji* (*Genji
Monogatari*) and *Myriad Leaves* (*Man'yōshū*),
the oldest collection of Japanese poems, as
examples of written works that depended
on *mono no aware*. *Genji* was written in the
eleventh century by Murasaki Shikubu, the
court name of the author, a woman distantly
related to the powerful Fujiwara family who
ruled Japan in the name of Heian-period
emperors. *Genji* is largely about the romantic
encounters of "the shining prince," and is rich
with poetic metaphors of longing, passion, and
sadness. *Genji* is one of the world's first novels,
as we know the genre today. In it, the word
aware appears on average once per page—a
total of 1044 times. The poems in the *Myriad
Leaves*, some 4500 of them collected over
more than 130 years ending in the middle of
the eighth century, are mostly love poems. At
the time they were written, men and women
had much more of an equal status, at least
compared with the later feudal period. Open
expression of emotion was not frowned upon
as it was later.

7.

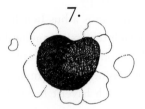

I HAVEN'T MENTIONED IT yet, but I had a reason for pausing my travels in Numazu. The village my grandfather left when he was a teenager is nearby. Katsuyama—"victory mountain"—isn't much of a town. I had trouble finding the place as it wasn't on the tourist map I first used to look for it. And I'm not one hundred percent sure it's really where my grandfather was born. The only reason that I know the village name is that it came up once when I was working for him that one summer. We were hacking away at overgrown bamboo in a customer's backyard and he said, "Lots of bamboo. Reminds me of Katsuyama."

"What's Katsuyama?"

"Little town where I came from in Japan. On the Izu Peninsula. Nothing much there." He told me what the name meant.

"How did it get that name?"

His machete thudded into an unruly stalk of bamboo. "Don't know."

That was our entire conversation. The "little town where I came from" didn't necessarily mean the town where he was born.

*

I TAKE THE TRAIN to Mishima then transfer to a local line which traverses the spine of the peninsula. The one-car train barely goes twenty miles an hour at top speed on the rails that twist between fields and through a valley.

Other than a couple of older women with shopping bags it's just me and the driver. I can only see the back of his head that bobs with the rhythm of the train. He announces the stops with a practiced, rhythmic chant that his passengers do not seem to appreciate. I wonder how he became the engineer of this mini-line and if he dreams of moving up the company hierarchy to driving one of the elite Shinkansen bullet trains. Has he resigned himself to his fate? Maybe he's perfectly happy.

The Katsuyama train station is a bus bench and an automated ticket dispenser. I get out and watch the train trundle down the tracks with the two passengers. The village consists of a couple of businesses and ten or twelve homes. One of the businesses is a small grocery store from what I can see through windows which haven't been cleaned lately. The largest building is an agricultural cooperative according to the rusting sign. A small flatbed truck is parked in the gravel yard next to the building. On the stone-paved entryway to the building are three pairs of rubber boots, caked with mud up to the ankle. They are lined up with toes pointing back to the street.

Laughter, guttural and male, floats toward me. It's hard to tell where the laughter is coming from as the sound echoes mutedly between the buildings. But I guess it's coming from the back of the co-op building. Instead of investigating the laughter, I first check out the store. There's a little wooden porch I have to step across to get to the door. The wood floorboards creak like something out of an old Western movie.

Someone inside the store screeches, "Quiet!"

Not the usual welcome in Japan.

Inside, a mustiness not covered by an incense stick burning in a little altar behind the front counter permeates the little store, the size of a living room. On one wall are four rows of shelving stacked with canned goods, bags of noodles, boxes of sugar, bottles of soy sauce, cello-wrapped dried fish and tiny shrimp. One of the shelves holds soap, shampoo, detergents, razors, and toilet paper. Along the other available wall is a cold unit, the glass front obscured by filmy condensation and scratches.

An elderly woman behind the counter mutters something and when I say "Excuse me?" she just cackles.

"Do you have any cold drinks?" I say in a loud clear voice. I don't know why I assume she is hard of hearing.

She steps around the counter, surprisingly spryly, and opens the cold unit. "Tea, soy milk, coffee, soda. Or do you need beer?"

I decide to eschew the alcohol and get a cold tea. "Tea, please. Just one."

She grabs a can out of the cold, takes it to the counter, and peers up at me.

"That's all," I say.

"One hundred ten yen."

As I dig for the coins, I ask her, "Is there anyone named Hara living here? I think my grandfather was born in Katsuyama."

"Just Hara? Not Takahara, or Sugihara?"

"Yes, just Hara."

"Nope. No Hara." She takes my coins and places the canned tea in a faded plastic bag from a department store.

"Thank you. How about Takahara?"

"No. No Takahara."

"Sugihara?"

"No Sugihara."

I can see where this is going so I take my tea, thank her, and leave.

When I go back to the co-op, it's quiet and the three pairs of boots are gone. I follow the road that goes through the village. A couple of dogs tethered on short ropes bark at me but no one comes out to see what the commotion might be about. The houses are old, with bleached wood siding, the roofs topped with gray tiles.

The road continues up the valley following a stream several feet across, too far to jump. The crops here aren't rice—some kind of root crop grows in the terraces created with rock and earthen embankments. I stop at the edge of one of the fields and bend down and poke at one of the young plants. A light green fleshy root shines brightly in the sun. Must be wasabi, the real wasabi, not the colored horseradish served at most sushi bars.

I walk along the stream bank coming to a place where it widens and slows. A deposit of rock is piled on a spit of sand. I climb down the bank and glance over the collection of polished rocks. There are all shapes and sizes from pebbles to bowling balls. A perfect spot to complete my next task of finding a pear-shaped rock.

As for the second task I've been assigned—the petty crime—I'm not sure how to go about that. Technically, I suppose, I'm committing a crime by working without having a proper visa. But that's not really a petty crime, like shoplifting a candy bar from a convenience store, or letting the air out of some car's tires. Something a juvenile delinquent would do.

I poke at the rocks for several minutes. I've narrowed my search criteria to size (pear sized) and general shape (round, not flat). Of course there are no rules, only objectives. My cold tea can is already empty and I wish I'd bought two or three. I think about tossing the can onto the stream bank, meeting my second task by littering. But while petty, it doesn't seem like much of a crime.

The rocks are starting to blur together, edges soften, three-dimensionality goes flat. I squat down and pick up fist-sized rocks, inspect them. None are pear-shaped. It might actually be difficult to find a pear-shaped rock. I could be here for days.

Well, not the kinds of pears we get back home, those tapered, curvy kinds of pears such as Bartlett, Anjou, Bosc. In Japan, a pear, *nashi*, is what we call an Asian pear, which is rounder, more like an apple. As soon as I realize this, I see a perfect *nashi*-shaped stone. With a whoop I grab it and hold it up in the air, triumphantly, an athlete with his gold medal.

Then I notice the three men on the bank staring at me, their rubber boots caked in mud. I lower my hand holding my rock and wave with the other. They stare at me for another moment then walk away.

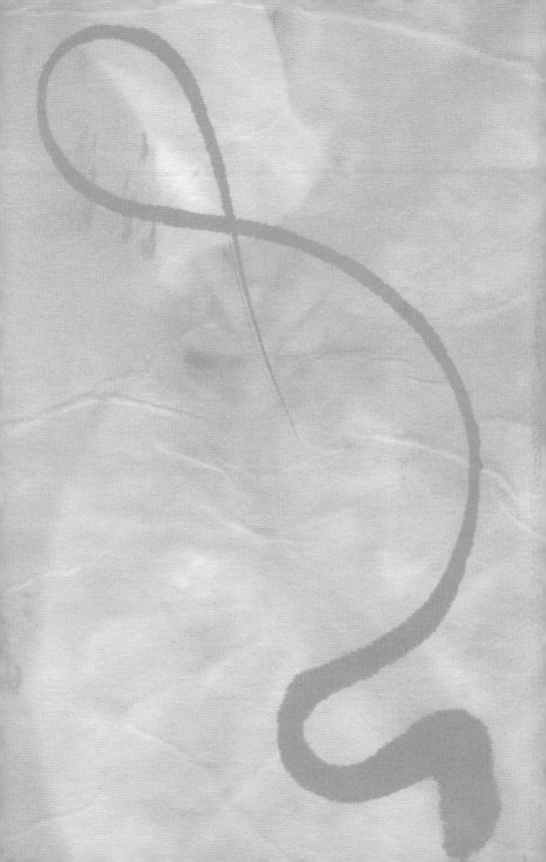

8.

AFTER MY LAST LESSON, the director of the English conversation school where I work calls me into his office. He's looking less than cheerful, not his casually confident self. Grim in fact. "Sensei, I have a problem," he says.

"Sorry to hear that, *shacho*." His name is Hiroyuki Yamada. He calls me sensei, an inside joke as I'm not really a sensei, that is, not a qualified teacher. Officially, I'm a "native speaker" who coaches students on American English pronunciation and idiom use. To return the sarcasm, I call him *shacho*—"company president." *Big* company president. Only a few years older than I am, he's married with a couple of young kids, owns a solid business, built his own house. A real grown-up in other words. And he's a good guy, although not above bending the employment and tax rules. Probably has to in order to make a living. I figure his problem has something to do with me.

"A national chain of language schools is trying to buy me out. They are trying to expand into new markets and eliminate the competition at the same time. The English language school business is becoming more cutthroat. Lower profit margins, fewer young people means fewer students."

"Congratulations," I say. "If the deal goes through then that's good for you, right? You'll probably make a lot of money."

Yamada says, "We haven't talked money yet. But, yes, they would have to pay a lot. Our school is successful and in a prime location. We have excellent instructors."

I guess what's bothering him. "This national chain has to play by the rules. No foreign teachers without the correct visa. No pay under the table. Or desk."

Yamada gives me a conspiratorial nod. "I'm not sure if this deal will go through. But we are beginning to negotiate and I will have to submit our accounting reports, our class lists, instructors. Naturally there will be questions about the visa status of our foreign teachers."

"Naturally. And if they find a problem, it might ruin the deal."

"It would definitely make our school less attractive to them. Or if the deal doesn't go through, and they know we pay foreign teachers off the books, they could make life uncomfortable for us."

I understand everything now. "If they can't buy you out, they'll run you out of town."

"It's a possibility."

I wait for him to ask me to resign from teaching. He gives me a smile, clearly wanting me to make the first move. I smile back. He keeps smiling. Finally, I just want to get away, have a beer. "All right," I say. "I don't want to mess up your deal. Just let me clear out my office."

Immediately, Yamada looks relieved. "You are a popular instructor. If the deal doesn't work out and they give up trying to start a school here I'll be happy to bring you back."

I don't think that'll ever happen.

He thanks me for my hard work and gives me my last pay envelope. It's already prepared so this was going to be my last day teaching no matter what. "With a little bonus," he says, slipping the envelope across his desk. On top of it.

*

AND I DO GO out for a drink, several. Kumiko and some of the other teachers and several students go with me. We end up at a funky little place near the school, appropriately named the American Bar and Grill. They proudly serve Bud and Miller, burgers and fries, meat loaf and mashed potatoes, apple pie. On the sound system, the Beach Boys, Aerosmith, and Britney Spears play incongruously.

I guess the other teachers and students think the food and American beer will comfort me. They're right. In a few minutes I'm feeling pretty good. I tell them, "I'm really going to miss spending hours preparing lessons, listening to you work your pronunciation, trying to pay attention to your stories about what you did over the weekend or on your company trips. I'm really going to miss how you struggle to explain the nuances of your culture."

They nod solemnly. My joking satire has failed.

Mr. Kono drunkenly shouts, "What's your hobby?"

Everyone cracks up.

They ask me what I'm going to do, if I'm going to leave Numazu. "I don't know," I answer. I really don't.

I don't want to leave Numazu yet. I'm having a good time with Kumiko although I'm not sure where it's going, if it has to go anywhere. Not everything has to go somewhere. In fact it's best if it doesn't. Once it gets there, whatever there is, then it's fully defined, no longer a mystery.

And then there's the professor. I'm intrigued by his experiment with me as guinea pig. I'm not sure what's going on with him either, but it's been the most interesting thing to happen to me for a while. So I want to let it ride. Besides, I still have one of his tasks to complete.

*

It's long past closing time. The bar owner locked the doors but hasn't kicked us out. Ten or twelve of us stragglers are laughing, talking, singing, and finishing the last, last round. In deference to me, I suppose, they are being casual, unscripted, untimed. Grateful, I pick at a piece of cold pizza, Japanese style with shrimp and corn. Kumiko is leaning against me, but then so is Mr. Kono.

Finally, spontaneously, we get up and head to the door. The bar owner is there with the bill. Everyone crowds around it, offering their share. When I try to pay, they all shake their heads, shout "no, no," and push me away.

Outside, we careen in all directions, Kumiko with me. She mumbles that she didn't know that Mr. Yamada was going to fire me. I mumble back that I know she didn't, that it didn't matter. She says "But I feel so guilty."

"No reason to."

"Akkk, it's not fair," she says in a slur of words.

Everyone feels worse about this than I do. "It's okay."

"You aren't going to leave, are you?"

"Leave? Not right away. I suppose eventually."

"No, I know that. Just not right away." She leans into me while we walk. I lean into her. A light mist starts falling and we make a run for my apartment.

*

WHILE KUMIKO SOAKS IN the tub I go out of the apartment and down the stairs to the second floor. On the landing, there is a storage closet that the bar uses. It's never locked, as I discovered when I checked a couple times. Inside the closet are stocks for the bar—cleaning supplies, linens and towels, boxes of snack foods, and a few extra bottles of booze.

No one's around. Reaching inside, I grab a bottle of whiskey and a couple of bags of peanuts then sprint back upstairs. Petty crime accomplished.

9.

WITH TIME ON MY hands, no place to be, I start to wallow around my apartment, as much as the tiny space will let me wallow. I don't see much of anyone except Kumiko once a week and usually only for a couple of hours. She's busy at her jobs, partly because she's teaching some of my classes.

The only other person I see is Professor Imai. He cancelled the rest of his lessons at the school, not so much out of loyalty, but that he wasn't impressed with the replacement options. I was the only one, apparently, who let him choose his topics and ramble on for his "lessons." The others wanted to instill didactic structure with vocabulary building, grammar exercises, and pronunciation drills. "I don't need any of that," he told me. No, he doesn't, I agreed.

He wants to continue meeting with me once a week as usual to discuss the prearranged topics. We meet in his office and he pays me what he paid the school, considerably more than I got paid by the school. I offered him a discount but he refused. On top of that, he hired me to edit his research papers he'd written in English for academic journals.

I found a couple of books in English about Japanese aesthetics with sections about Motoori Norinaga. They make for interesting reading while I sit in a Mos Burger, slowly eating a rice burger, drinking soy milk. The high school girls who work there whisper about me. I think they are kind of scared of me. What kind of weird guy sits in a Mos Burger for hours tapping notes into his laptop or reading a book—a book that's not a manga? I'm sure they think I'm homeless or will soon exhibit some other antisocial behavior.

While I was at the Mos Burger earlier, I heard two customers talking about another Aokigahara suicide. A police officer patrolling the edges of the forest spotted a parked car. When he got close to it he could see the tape sealing the seams of the windows and doors. He looked inside, saw three occupants making preparations to light the charcoal. The officer banged on the window, yelled at them to open the door. Instead, one of them took out a knife and slit the throats of the other two, then stabbed himself in the neck, opening his jugular.

*

PROFESSOR IMAI HANDS ME a draft of one of his papers. *Toward a Theory of Mutable and Immutable Personality Traits* is nearly two hundred pages. While I flip through it, he shakes his head sadly. "It needs a lot of work. I get bogged down in long complex sentences, as if I'm lost and don't know where to turn. I know what I'm thinking, but the words get stuck, twisted."

I've noticed the professor's logic does get a little confused in long sentences. "I'll give it my best effort. It might take me two weeks."

"Take your time."

"I appreciate you giving me the work."

"I'm sorry it's not more."

"No, it's fine." And it is. I can pay a month's rent with it and not have to dip too far into my travel funds.

He relaxes back into his chair. "Did you accomplish your next two tasks?"

From my backpack, I take out the Asian pear-shaped rock, a label from a bottle of whiskey, and two empty peanut packs.

The professor says as he picks up the rock, "It really does look like a pear, don't you think? Where did you find it?"

"Along a stream in Katsuyama."

The professor nods. "Ah, Katsuyama. Years ago I took a trip to a hot springs resort in Meijiro, a town one stop away from Katsuyama. Why did you choose to look there?"

"I believe my grandfather was born in Katsuyama. Or at least he lived there at one time."

The professor wraps the stone in both hands as if it's an egg. "Then the stone is of great importance to you."

"I don't know if it is. Why did you want to me to find a stone shaped like a pear?"

"The action and reaction is important. How did you feel when you found it?"

"It took a long time for me to find it." I explain how I changed my focus from a typical pear found in the US to an Asian pear. "I yelled something. Some farmers came over to look at the crazy guy holding a rock."

"Interesting. I hadn't thought of the different species of pear." He places the stone on the desk then shifts to the whiskey label and peanut bags. "And your petty crime?"

I tell him about the bar's storage closet. "Is that what you had in mind?"

"I had nothing specific in mind but your crime does fulfill the task's objectives."

"And the reasons are the same? Action and reaction?"

"Exactly. What was your reaction?"

"I felt elation as with the stone. But it was tempered with guilt. Even though I find their karaoke system irritating, I felt badly about stealing from the bar."

"That makes sense," the professor says in a flat monotone that sounds more like disinterest or distraction.

I change the subject. "Did you hear about the suicide yesterday at Aokigahara?"

He nods. "Very messy result. You seem curious about Aokigahara. That's where you went for the first task."

"I find it difficult to understand why someone would want to commit suicide in such a ritualistic, almost artistic, way. Everything planned to the detail. Even in this case, they had a plan in case they were discovered before they could carry it out."

The professor touches the rock, rolls it with his fingertips. "Many suicides are not merely trying to end the pain in their lives, they want to make a statement. For most, their suicide is the ultimate act of their lives. The act they will be remembered for." He looks at me, his English teacher.

"Or should I say, the act for which they will be remembered."

"Either," I say. "The latter is more formal. Only real sticklers demand no prepositions at the end of a sentence."

The professor closes his eyes briefly, making a mental grammar note. "Many suicides are unsuccessful in their lives, or rather they believe they are unsuccessful. They want the suicide act to show they can be successful. So they go to extraordinary measures to ensure it happens. And that it happens in a sensational way."

After a long pause, I change the subject and ask the professor for my next task.

He claps his hand on the pear-shaped stone. "Your next task is to go to the site of the recent suicide. Find something, a tree, a plant, a view that would have been the last thing the victims might have seen. Write a poem about it. Or create a work of art. Some expression of what they might have felt."

The word "aesthetic" comes from the Greek
word meaning "of sense perception." As René
Descartes ("I think, therefore I am") might
say, "I perceive, therefore I feel." We cannot
help but feel when we perceive; much of these
correlations between the external world and
our feelings are hard-wired from birth, rather
than learned. For example, infants have an
instilled fear of heights without having to fall
a few times to get the message that falling
from a great height is not a good idea. Other
studies show that infants react more positively
to people whose faces are more symmetrical
than to those with even slight asymmetries.
Unlike sweet food, sour foods are an acquired
taste, our initial negative response possibly
evolved from sourness indicating spoiled foods.

10.

I TAKE THE BUS to Takegawa, a town at the edge of Aokigahara Forest. Several military men and a few women are walking around the main street. American military I should clarify, young Marines from a nearby base. They look a lot younger when they are out of their uniforms. They have bad haircuts and fierce tattoos on their arms. The locals must be used to seeing them because they don't give the Marines a second glance. Sometimes the Marines get down into Numazu, strolling the streets for inexpensive souvenirs, eating at McDonald's and KFC, frequenting the discos and American-style bars. They must think I'm Japanese and don't understand English because when I happen to be in earshot they say some pretty crude things about the locals. Well, not all of the Marines do this. Actually, probably only a few.

I stop at a convenience store, grab a bottle of water and an energy bar. I pay for them, as I'm no longer committing petty crimes. Since I'm the only customer I ask the clerk, a cheery looking young guy, maybe twenty, twenty-two, if he heard about the latest suicide at Aokigahara.

"Hey," he says, "Are you from America?"

"How did you know?" I think I speak pretty good Japanese.

"Your accent. I'm good at detecting accents. Say something in English."

I rattle off my question in English.

He cocks his head and says, "Southern California?"

A pretty good trick. "How did you know that?"

"I study accents. I can discern all regional dialects in Japan, and now I'm studying America. We get a lot of Americans in here so I've been tuning my ear. My skill doesn't have much value but it's a good conversation starter with strangers. So what do you want to know about the suicide last week? More importantly, why?"

"I'm writing an article about the suicides in Aokigahara."

"Are you a journalist or an academic?"

"I'm a researcher for a psychology professor."

"Most of the locals don't want to talk about the suicides. It's not something they want to be famous for."

"How about you? Don't want to talk about it either?"

He shrugs. "I don't mind. What do you want to know?"

"Where did it happen exactly for a start. I'd like to go to the actual scene."

He scratches the back of his head. "That was their mistake. They stopped right off the main road. They should have gone back in further. Everyone knows the cops are patrolling. Well, usually patrolling. Some of them just go up the forest and take a nap." On the back of a receipt, the clerk sketches me a map.

"Thanks. Is it true they cut their own throats?"

"That's what I heard. Of course I didn't see it with my own eyes."

"Were they from around here?"

"No. Two from Tokyo, one from Nagoya."

"They came far to commit suicide."

The clerk shrugs. "It's Aokigahara. Like it or not, it's the most famous spot in Japan for suicide."

*

IT TAKES ME ABOUT twenty minutes to walk to the suicide spot. Just off the main road there is a turnoff onto a narrow road that I recognize. It's the same farm road I found when I was lost. A kilometer or so up the road is the field where I ran into the farmer. I sit on a guard rail post and sketch in that geographical information, including the terraced fields and stream. When I remember the shrine, I mark it too. I'm sure my scale is way off, and I'm not sure why I feel the need to add my personal knowledge to the map. It just seems incomplete without it.

There's still some evidence of the suicide: sets of tire marks in the soft ground, gravel spewed across the asphalt, four official stakes marking the spot where a car was parked. I look around to find something that they might have seen in their last moments alive. Of course the last views would have been the inside of the car, a police officer pounding on the window, the blade of a knife. But in the moments before that, they might have looked out the car, taking in the scenery for the last time.

Standing in the marked spot, I can see the sky. Of course, that might be obscured by the car roof. I lower my gaze and follow a dense stand of trees up a slope to a rock outcropping. A lone tree, some type of pine, is growing out of the rocks at a severe angle, its roots exposed and gripping the rocks.

That's the last thing I would have seen if I'd been in the car. I make a sketch of the tree and snap a photo. I jot down a few thoughts, the beginnings of a poem, in a notebook.

Before I go back into town, I walk along the farm road toward the little, makeshift shrine. For an unknown reason, I'm drawn back to it, wanting to absorb its details, maybe sketch it too.

When I get to where the shrine should be, I can't find it. I poke around the brush in widening circles in case I'm off a few feet. Finally, I find a bare spot on the ground. I'm sure this is where the shrine should be, just off the path roughly between a rock and a tree. Looking closely at the ground, I can tell the scraping marks were made with the flat blade of a shovel.

On the ~~brink~~ verge of falling
A lone pine ~~grips~~ clings to the cliff
Afraid to look down

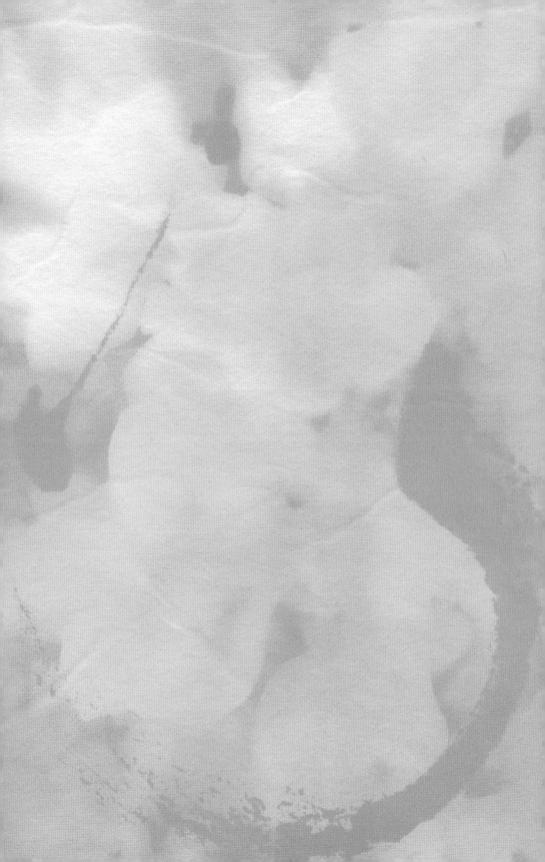

11.

IT'S A HOLIDAY WEEKEND. Which means nothing to me of course but Kumiko has the weekend off. I suggest we go to a hot-springs resort, the one in the town of Meijiro mentioned by the professor. She starts with all sorts of excuses. The expense, it's too late to get a reservation anywhere, the stress of her job interviews won't let her relax. I counter with sound rebuttals. I already called the inn the professor mentioned and made a reservation, and I received a bonus from the professor (sort of true, he paid for a dinner). To counter her final excuse I come up with the maxim that it's impossible *not* to relax at a hot-springs inn.

She sighs and agrees.

*

WE PASS THROUGH KATSUYAMA on the way to Meijiro. I mention that I believe my grandfather was born in the village.

"In this little place?"

"Is it hard to believe?"

"I mean it's hard to believe anyone could be from such a small place."

I still don't understand.

She thinks a moment and tries, this time in Japanese, "It seems like the kind of place … if you were born there you'd never leave."

*

WE CHECK INTO THE inn in the late afternoon. Sleepy from the journey, we take a nap. We wake up just in time for dinner served in our room. After, we soak in the outdoor hot-springs bath down a little hill from the inn. The moon is just a sliver and the water is black, the steam rising off the water is like a low cloud. A poet could write a nice little poem about the scene.

A few other couples are in the water, all of us clutching little white towels. Mine is covering a hard-on. Kumiko brushes her hand against it and giggles. We get out and dry off, slip on the *yukata* robes, and hurry back to our room, the wooden geta slippers clomping out gobs of sound on the stone path.

In our room, the futon is already made up and we throw off our *yukata*, jump onto the futon. Our moist, plumped skin heated further with friction. When we finish and I'm drifting off, I hear her softly crying into her pillow.

Oh.

*

WE ONLY SPEND ONE night at the Meijiro hot springs inn before we return to Numazu. Kumiko says she is relaxed and ready to get to work. I don't know if she's telling the truth. Nor do I ask why she was crying. I have the feeling she doesn't want to talk about it.

Back in my apartment, I check emails and get one from Carine. She's coming to old Nippon for a week-long visit. We had talked about a visit after I settled in Numazu but I didn't think she'd ever get around to it. The possibility of a visit hadn't come up in our emails for months. Her life is as full as usual (yes, even *sans moi*) with work and friends. She emails me tidbits: a friend's unexpected pregnancy, her promotion from Creative Associate to Senior Creative Associate at her design firm, the parties she held or attended—describing in detail those requiring costumes, or at least severe makeup. The kind of parties I usually managed to avoid, begging off with a spare excuse.

She doesn't mention a love life, so I assume she has one.

If I were in L.A. now, what would I be doing? Let's see ... final proof-checking the water tower manual, going cross-eyed, chugging coffee, maintaining a sugar high. I'd take the galleys home with me, spread the pages on my coffee table and sit on the floor, back against the sofa, blue pencil in hand, the stereo on low. The music would be classical or acid jazz, nothing with words. No earful to interfere with the eyeful.

More than boring and tedious, however, the imagined scene had a comfortable feel to it.

Reality: I'm on my futon, propped up against my pillows, an overwrought soapy drama on the TV. Crazily, I'm yelling at the naive housewife, bored out of her skull, getting sucked into an affair with her gym instructor, a guy who, unknown to the heroine, beat up his previous fling at the gym.

While I'm watching/not-watching the inevitable drama of abuse unfolding (will she kill him in self defense, get rid of the body, hide the evidence?), I'm working on my assignment from the professor. I bought pencils with soft and hard graphite, a handful of colored markers, a pad of sketch paper, a beginner's calligraphy set. I'm not much of an artist, although I did go through a youthful phase of copying characters in the funnies. I was pretty good at copying, not good at creating my own images. All this happened in a short couple of years, about age twelve to fourteen. I don't recall if I was withdrawing (so to speak) into an imaginary world, to escape my gawky, scrawny body, weird skin, and beginnings of a bad mustache. I don't think so. I started doing it for no reason, then stopped doing it for no reason.

To satisfy my assigned task, I chose the art option because as poor an artist as I am, I'm a worse poet. I suppose it's because of my documented lack of emotional intelligence. Poetry pares human existence into kernels of emotion. A deep understanding of the human perception/reaction cycle is crucial to writing poetry. Wait a minute … didn't I just read that in the professor's paper?

But even if I rated high on the emotional intelligence scale, I doubt if I could write a decent poem. Too many years of technical writing, of deadly clear and concise exposition. Subject/verb/object, no more, no less. Poetry requires a different kind of ear for language than I have. The poetic language has to stand out, unlike technical writing that tries to fade away, the only thing left transparent meaning.

Wait … as I guessed, the housewife stabs her gym fling in the heart with scissors. There's surprisingly little blood, but now she's got that hefty gym-fling's body to deal with.

I've got a couple of drawings completed of the tree clinging to the cliff face, one's actually not too bad. I spent a lot of time working on precise rendering of the exposed roots. They are what give the scene power, where life begins and ends.

But still I'm not satisfied. It's too literal, too obvious. I get up and go the couple of steps into the kitchen. I grab a cold can of green tea from the mini fridge, say "hi" to one of the roaches giving me the eye, not one skittish bone in its body worried I'd try to kill it. Well, actually, and now the technical writer speaking, a cockroach's skeleton is *outside* its body.

Back on my futon, bending over and admiring my work, a fat drop of condensation from the can falls right in the middle of the art. The colors blend and spread, softening the image. Damn. Oh well. I let more drips fall. Is this how Jackson Pollock got the idea for his drip paintings?

When the last drip falls, it's not just a muddled mess, it's how the clinging tree would really be seen, blurred and runny, through dying eyes.

*

THE TV DRAMA PLAYS out like this: the wife/murderer bundles up the gym fling's body in a futon cover and drags it into the bedding closet. Her husband never sets out the futon at night, so she figures the body is safely hidden. She cleans up the mess and sets dinner on the table just as hubby comes home. He's dragging himself through the house, complaining of a cold or the flu and just wants to go to bed. He reaches for the bedding closet … okay, to make a long story short, she keeps hubby away from the body and the next day drags it to her car, drives outside of Tokyo, and dumps it in a canal. It looks like she's in the clear until the body is discovered. A suave and super-intuitive detective finds a single thread of Spandex fiber on the body. Improbably, he traces it to her. Breaking her down, gently, the detective understands she destroyed a monster. The fiber evidence disappears, her confession forgotten, and she gazes at the detective lovingly.

*

KUMIKO COMES OVER AFTER her last lesson. She sighs when I ask if she wants to go out. "Sorry, it's been a long day. Can we stay in?"

I rub the back of her neck while I guide her to the futon. "Relax. I'll go get us some drinks and sushi from the 7-Eleven."

"Okay. But be careful."

"Careful? In the 7-Eleven?"

"When I was at the school a police detective was talking with the school director, asking about a 'suspicious' foreigner hanging around town. I couldn't hear everything he said, but a bar complained about missing food and bottles of alcohol."

That's an exaggeration. I only took one bottle. "Was this police detective suave and super-intuitive?"

"Huh?"

"Never mind."

"He was also saying something about foreigners with no visas trying to get teaching jobs."

*

WHEN I GET BACK, successful in avoiding detection, Kumiko is looking through my sketches and finished art work.

"What's this?" she asks.

If I have to tell her, then I've failed as an artist. "Just messing around. I used to draw when I was younger."

She studies the piece treated with water drops. "Interesting."

We eat and drink mostly in silence. She regains some energy and cleans up the dinner mess: foam containers, cellophane, single shoyu packs, disposable chopsticks. She opens another beer, refills our glasses, and says, "I'm going to Tokyo for a month. Interviews and a trial period with the publishing company."

"Congratulations. That's great. I'm really happy for you."

She sips from her glass, not looking at me.

12.

I ASK THE PROFESSOR, "Is the Japanese view of suicide different from, say, the American view?" We are finished going through my editing suggestions on several pages of his paper. In his office, on a side table, several stacks of articles and papers are arranged in categories. Yellow tongues of sticky notes mark pages of interest. All correlated to the references cited in his paper.

The professor taps his cheek. "Suicide is not my area of expertise but I assume your underlying question asks if suicide is more accepted here than in Western countries? Historically, suicide here was often required in matters of dishonor. That's no longer the case, although dishonor remains a reason. Regardless of the past, however, the government views a relatively high suicide rate as a pressing problem. It's about four times the rate in the U.S., I believe. Although less than half of Russia's and other old Soviet bloc countries. On the other hand, the same question could be asked about homicide rates. Japan has one of the lowest rates in the world. More than ten times less than the U.S."

"True. More like a hundred times if you're a black male. And probably five hundred times higher if you're a black male in some areas of Los Angeles."

"So can we say that homicide is more accepted in the U.S. because the rate is so much higher? No, of course not. The point is there are many complicating factors."

I nod in agreement. "The point is also we can't draw general conclusions merely because the rates are different. Not without understanding the context in which they occur."

He smiles. "You've been reading my paper while you edit."

"Hard not to."

"Why do you ask about suicide? Are you still fascinated with Aokigahara?"

I'm not sure fascinated is the correct word. Certainly not obsessed. More like it correlates with my interest in understanding the victim's pain. "It's hard for me to understand why they would commit suicide. I'm sure this has something to do with my lack of *mono no aware*."

The professor says nothing for a while. "It's difficult to say. Killing oneself is incomprehensible to most people. Not until you are in that person's situation, feeling what he or she feels, can you understand the desire to end one's own life."

"There can be no empathy?"

"Sympathy perhaps, Empathy no."

That's a very subtle difference. "That reminds me, I did my drawing for my next task." I pull out a folder from my bag and open it on the professor's desk. I'd completed a few more of the water-splash works.

"Hmm," he says.

"Don't tell me. It's 'interesting.' So it's not so good?"

"It is good. It's a matter of expression. If I may hazard a guess, you used this kind of blurring technique to show the view from a dying person."

"That's how it turned out anyway." I explain the accidental drips.

"Did creating the art affect your emotional outlook for the Aokigahara suicide victims?"

"I suppose not," I say after thinking about it.

"Interesting," says the professor, neither disappointed nor surprised, simply matter-of-fact.

*

THE PROFESSOR BEGS OFF with an early evening. He seems tired, perhaps from the editing, perhaps from our discussion of suicide. I'm not feeling tired and after being cooped up in my apartment most of the day working on the professor's paper, I'm ready for some action. Not sure what kind of action and without my students and without Kumiko, I realize I'm out of friends.

Walking along the strip of bars near the train station but not seeing anyplace I'd enjoy, I stop in the professor's bar.

Mama-san gives me a big welcome when I enter the bar, although her greeting lacks the tinge of friendship she gives the professor. Her greeting for him is a kind of a softening and lengthening of "*Irasshai.*" It's subtle but I can pick up on it.

As I make my way to the far stool at the bar, the other customers give me a glance as if I'm an intruder in their private club. The bar has a different vibe without the professor, likely because I'm more obviously the outsider that I am.

Who cares? Mama-san serves me a beer—luckily I can pass on the whiskey-water the professor insists on ordering for me. I can't, however, get away from the small plate of chicken livers she serves. Not a huge fan of chicken livers.

When there's a lull, she asks what the professor is up to. "He had to work late," I say. I don't know why I don't tell her the truth.

"He will be here later?"

"I don't know. I don't think so."

"Okay," she says and goes to check on the others in the bar.

The professor gave me a new task. Apparently not satisfied with my artistic rendition of the suicide scene he asks me to write a poem. About what? I asked him. He said, "I know you came to Japan to discover some of your grandfather's life here. How is that going?"

I told him about Katsuyama and not finding anything there. He suggested that I go back and try to find some memory—maybe remembrance is a better word—of my grandfather. When I've found it, he assigns me the task of writing a poem about the remembrance.

It seems like a difficult task. Not just because of my poetry skills. My grandfather left Japan such a long time ago. Surely, anyone who would have known him would be dead. And I know only a little about his side of the family. I have a vague recollection of an old genealogical chart. I should email my uncle, my dad's oldest brother, who keeps a box of my grandfather's papers and ask him to send a copy.

After a brief, weak protest, I agree to the task. Not so much because I think I can overcome my poetic deficiency, but I need to get away from Numazu for a while. Without Kumiko, without a job other than the editing, it's getting a little boring. Not to mention the police scrutiny.

I'm pretty sure there isn't any place to stay in Katsuyama. I could stay at the Meijiro hot springs inn. It would be a little expensive, but relaxing.

*

I'M LINGERING IN THE bar, the last customer, finishing up another beer and a bowl of mountain potato stew, waiting until the time when the karaoke machine gets turned off back home. Mama-san asks if I need anything else.

"No thank you, I'll be out of your hair soon."

"Please, don't hurry."

Between bites and sips we chat about the professor. "How long has he been a customer?"

She smiles and looks to his favorite seat. "He was one of my first customers. More than twenty years ago. He'd just gotten his job at the university. He didn't know anyone in town."

"Twenty years … you've gone through a lot together."

She raises an eyebrow. "Yes. I suppose so."

When she doesn't offer any specifics I say, "He never talks about his personal life. Never lets our conversations become small talk. I don't even know if he's married."

Mama-san nods. "He is a serious type." After a hesitation, she says, "But I will tell you he's divorced and doesn't like to talk about it." She pours the last of my beer into the glass.

"He seems distracted," I say. "Do you know if anything is wrong?"

"Nothing that I know about."

*

ON THE WAY HOME, without thinking, I pass by the police box near the train station. Out of the corner of my eye I see a night-duty police officer glance up and watch me pass.

13.

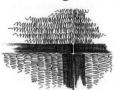

I'M WALKING FROM THE train station in Meijiro to the hot springs inn. The road winds underneath a canopy of tree tops. It rained earlier so drops slide off the leaves and plunk me on the head. The asphalt is shiny and slick, the air wet, fresh. I could have taken a taxi from the station or called the inn for a ride but I'm in no hurry.

Apparently it's not the norm to be checking into a hot springs inn as a single. When I made the reservation, I had a hard time getting it across that I wanted a room for three nights for myself. The proprietress apparently thought it was one room for three, *insisted* it must be one room for three. When it was clear what I meant, she became suspicious, asking me what I was intending to do there for three nights by myself. Just relaxing, my answer, did not seem to satisfy her. I have no idea what kinds of mischief she thought I might be capable of. I found out later that the inns are traditionally for either couples or company groups.

She eventually made the reservation when I explained I stayed there only a few weeks ago with my girlfriend. She remembered me and apologized for questioning me.

The proprietor and proprietress greet me with a bow and a hearty welcome when I walk through the inn's front door. She bows deeply and apologizes again. Her husband wears his thick, black-framed glasses, oddly fashionable on him. He takes my bag and places it by the front desk. He hands me a warm, damp face towel to freshen up while he says that he would have picked me up at the train station if I had only called.

"It's okay," I say. "It was a nice walk."

He looks mystified by that for a moment but laughs heartily, disposes my used towel, grabs my bag, and motions me to follow. We walk down the long corridor with the rooms and stop at the end. He nods at the door, opens it and bows as I pass him to enter the room. It's a corner room with a view of the stream that is below the inn. I'm pretty sure it's the same stream that flows through Katsuyama, the stream where I found the pear-shaped rock.

He places my bag on the floor and shows me how to open the sliding paper door to reveal the garden path to the outdoor hot springs. He introduces me to the bathroom: demonstrates the hot and cold faucets, where the *yukata* are hanging. Shows me again the sliding door.

I step up and slide the door in and out. "Marvelous," I say. "You built these?"

He gives me a modest nod. "Dinner is at seven."

When he leaves, I lie down on the mat floor and fall right asleep.

*

I'M HALFWAY THROUGH DINNER—several small plates of fish, veggies, an egg custard with shrimp, rice, served in my room by one of the inn's maids. She says nothing to me, doesn't look at me directly. She must be scared of the single male staying for three nights.

I slept the afternoon away. I had wanted to do a little exploring around the area, check out the possibilities of a presence of my grandfather. I wasn't sure how I was going to do that. Just start asking around, I guess.

But the long nap felt good.

The proprietor stops by, bringing a bottle and two sake cups. "It's a rough local sake," he says pouring me a glass full.

I return the favor by filling his cup. We toast and down the sake in one gulp. It's very good. When I tell him that he shakes his head. "Just a rough local sake," he tells me again.

We have another glass and then another.

He takes off his glasses, wipes the lens, inspects the heavy black frames.

"Where is the lovely woman you came with last time?"

"She's moved to Tokyo for a month. Maybe longer."

"Ah, love lost," he says sadly.

I don't tell him he's drawn the wrong conclusion. Of course he may be right.

He returns his glasses to their perch and scratches his belly. "What do you do?"

Good question. What *do* I do? "Right now, I'm just traveling around Japan."

"You must be Japanese American," he says.

"Yes. Actually, I think my grandfather was born in Katsuyama."

"Katsuyama?" His wide but sparse eyebrows arch up to the middle of his forehead. He leans forward, looks outside, and points upstream. "That Katsuyama?"

I tell him as much as I know about my grandfather and Katsuyama.

"Hara is your family name?"

I nod.

He closes his eyes and mumbles my name a few times. "Don't know any Hara. When was he born?"

"We believe it was 1909, although no one is exactly sure."

He translates it into the Japanese system: "Meiji forty-one." He clucks his tongue and repeats, "Meiji forty-one."

"Does that mean anything?"

He shrugs. "Not to me."

*

WE'VE ALMOST FINISHED THE entire bottle of the rough, local sake. I've got a good buzz, no, a great buzz. The sake is smooth, no doubt expensive.

"What did you do in America? What kind of work?"

"I was a writer and editor. Science and technology."

"Ahh, a writer. Great! A few famous poets and writers have stayed here. This inn is over four-hundred years old, you know." He lists a few of the famous literary guests. I don't recognize any of them, not that I would expect to. I know a few famous Japanese writers. The only poet I would know by name is Basho, the haiku writer.

"Are you a poet?" I ask my host.

He gives me another of his modest responses, this time waving his hand in front of his face several times like he is fanning away the heat. "I am only a poor *amateur*," he says. The last word is in English.

"I'd like to read some of your poems. Another of my reasons for coming here is that I need to write a poem."

"A poem? About what?"

"I hope to find something about my grandfather, some memory of him. Then write a poem about that."

He gives me a friendly, conspiratorial smile. "So you are more than just a technical writer."

"No. I've never written a poem before."

"Never?"

"Well, I've messed around a little, trying out haiku. But I lack *mono no aware*."

The proprietor looks surprised. "You know *mono no aware*? Not many people know about it. Then you know about Motoori Norinaga."

"A little."

"Most Japanese know nothing about him. I have a copy of his works. My favorite is *The Sedge Hat Diary*. It's about a trip he made to the Yoshino area in Nara Prefecture. It's a simple account, really, but shows his considerable knowledge and insight."

"I'd like to read it," I say. "But I'm very slow at reading Japanese."

"I'll let you borrow it. And because you know about *mono no aware*, I would be happy to let you read a few of my poor poems."

He pours me another cup of sake. I return the favor. The bottle is empty. We stare at it.

It rained, often heavily, during the first two days
of Norinaga's journey. Norinaga found the rain
to be sad, inspiring a poem: "Yesterday, today/
it rained off and on—/how difficult/for the
clouds to clear:/Spring rains in Kataka."

Staying in Meijiro, searching the past
for a living memory,
the rain is good
for sleeping off a bottle of sake.

14.

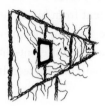

SOMEONE IS KNOCKING ON the door to my room and all I want to do is sleep. Now someone is in my room saying, "Good morning. Breakfast."

I open a crusted eye. The proprietress, ever smiling, is on her knees in front of the table setting out breakfast.

Propping up on one elbow, I check out the food. It's a traditional breakfast: miso soup, squares of roasted nori, fried whole sweet fish, raw egg, rice. Of course, they would serve a traditional breakfast, it's a traditional inn.

The best thing on the table is the green tea. I'm parched, dehydrated from all the sake. I suck down a cup of tea as soon as she pours it.

As if reading my mind, she says, "Did you enjoy the sake last night?"

"It was very delicious."

"My husband was such a pest last night. I scolded him for bothering you."

"No, I enjoyed his company." Then I remember he was going to give me some of his poems and Norinaga's writings. I spot a stack of books and journals just inside the door.

She sees where I'm looking and shakes her head. "You don't have to read his awful poetry."

I laugh. "It's okay, I want to."

She sighs and says, "He has big ambitions. Don't pay him any attention."

*

BREAKFAST AND A LONG soak energize and relax me at the same time. When I
return from the hot springs, my room is cleaned, a new flower arrangement
on the table. I get dressed and before I take off to search for my grandfather's
memory, I open the first notebook of the proprietor's poems. Written in
elegant calligraphy on the title page is a name: Johei. It must be his poetic
pseudonym because it's different from his name on his business card.

I read what I can of the first few poems about the moon, the river,
cedars, night sounds. One is a little different—it's about a person, I assume
a man, his thoughts, and the path of a meteor. It catches my eye because it
uses the word *aware*.

> *A man, full of deep feelings (aware)*
> *watches a falling star*
> *light the sky*
> *but feels nothing.*

I'm not sure I've captured the subtlety of the poem in the translation, but
that's the general idea.

As I'm leaving the inn, the book and poetry in my day pack, the
proprietor catches up with me. "Good morning," he says. "Sorry I kept you
up so long last night."

"No need to apologize."

He glances over his shoulder then whispers, "According to my wife
I do."

"No, no, I enjoyed the conversation and the sake."

He looks pleased.

"And thank you for the book and poetry." I open my bag for him to
inspect. "You don't mind if I take them with me to look at during the day."

He shakes his head vigorously. "No please do."

"I've read a few poems already and find them excellent."

He blushes. "No, they are not good."

"No, they are very good. Thank you for letting me read them."

He shakes his head again. "Thank you for reading them."

I'm a little tired of the back and forth here, so I start to move toward the door. He says, "Just a minute. I have a name of someone who might help you." He goes to the front desk and writes on a slip of paper. He hands it to me. "Setsuko Yone works at the municipal museum, she's young but knows much of the history of the area."

I thank him, he thanks me, and so on.

*

THE MUSEUM'S ARCHITECTURE IS surprisingly modern, with curved glass, burnished aluminum, raw concrete. I was expecting to see an historic, preserved building. Inside, the lobby is spacious, larger than what it looks like it should be from the outside. The woman seated at the reception desk welcomes me. Instead of asking to see Setsuko Yone right away, I pay the entrance fee, get a brochure describing the exhibits.

The main exhibits show the chronological history of the area from prehistory to current day. Other displays show the region's agriculture past, historic figures who'd been born in the area or passed through, and the numerous hot springs inns. There is a display of the inn where I'm staying— one enlarged photo shows it during the late 1800s. The inn hasn't changed at all.

Finished, I go back to the front and ask to see Setsuko Yone. The front desk receptionist looks hesitant, then I show her the paper from the inn proprietor and she calls on her phone. In a few seconds the "Employees Only" door opens.

Setsuko Yone is young, maybe my age or a year or two older. She dresses stylish and professionally. She wears understated glasses; the frames are thin gold wires. We quickly introduce ourselves.

In her meticulous office, she listens to my story. When I finish, she taps her pen on a pad of paper. "Your grandfather was born in 1909 and arrived in America which year?"

"I think he was fifteen or sixteen, so it was 1924 or 1925."

"The end of the Taisho Era," she says. "And you're sure it's Katsuyama?"

"That's what he told me. Katsuyama on the Izu Peninsula."

"And don't forget about the bamboo grove," she says, with a lilt of sarcasm.

"I realize it's not much to go on."

"You've tried at the family registrar's office, I assume?"

"No, I'm not sure how to do that."

"The large building across the street is the municipal hall. Ask in Family Records for your grandfather's birth records in Katsuyama. In the meantime, I'll check here for any records and research the history of the area from 1909 through 1925. Can you return tomorrow?"

After my profuse apology for taking up her time with such a trivial matter, I thank her and leave. Outside the air is fresh, damp, full of green smells, as if nature is closing in on me.

Nature's influence on japanese literature goes back considerably far in the country's history. Ancient Buddhist art, for example, illustrates an iconic, universal view firmly placing humankind in a symbiotic relationship with nature. This view contrasts with other views placing humans above or as masters of nature. The early Japanese artist and writer followed *mono no aware* (though that label was not applied until Norinaga's time) as norms or rules that guide Japanese behavior, based on this deep affinity with nature and beauty, and a spontaneous, emotional response to them.

15.

DINNER IS SERVED AND the proprietor poet arrives furtively with another bottle of sake. As he opens the bottle, my mouth waters in a Pavlovian response. He asks how I succeeded with my task.

"Very well. Thank you for the introduction to Setsuko Yone. She was very helpful. I'm going back to the museum tomorrow to talk again with her. Unfortunately, I couldn't find any information at the family registrar's office. They have no records of anyone with my grandfather's name."

After my failure with the family registrar I walked around the town and found a path along the stream leading toward Katsuyama. I walked for several minutes until I reached a bamboo grove. I wandered in its dark and quiet for a few minutes.

I headed back toward Meijiro and found a noodle restaurant in the town. Over a bowl of steaming ramen and a pot of tea, I read from the proprietor's notebook. After that I walked around town and bought some silly souvenirs—a miniature cedar tree, packets of bath salts—for whom, I don't know.

"I read some more of your poems," I tell him. "I like them very much. Have you published them?"

His smile disappears behind embarrassment. "No, no. Well, only one." He opens one of the journals he lent me, flips through the pages, and turns it toward me. "This one."

It's a poem about a man fishing, seeing his reflection, not recognizing himself, then thinking he's a fish. Casting his line toward the image, the reflection disappears in the ripples. Underneath is a note: Published in the 1973 Spring issue of *Contemporary Poetry.*

When I look up, he takes a drink of sake as if washing down his only success.

"Why did you start writing poetry?" I ask him.

"I worked as a government accountant for five years before marrying into the family who owns the inn. I started writing poetry when I was in the accounting office, I suppose, to balance my life of numbers with words. I'm happy with my poetry." He gazes outside, then belches. That makes us laugh. Waving his hands to quiet me, he says, "A man, contemplating his navel, satisfied, belches."

I smile at his spontaneous poem. He points at me. My turn. "Uh, um," I mumble while trying to think of something. Finally I come up with: "A man full of sake, tries to write a poem, but can only write, 'uh, um, uh, um.'"

*

WE SPAR WITH POEMS until the bottle of sake is dry and, as we did the night before, we can only stare at it. The sparring reminds me of the one time I tried to learn a Japanese martial art. I lasted only two months. I wasn't a stellar student for many reasons but the sensei summed up my difficulties this way: "You think too much and not enough." Another mystical aphorism to puzzle out, I thought at the time. There had been many of them, such as "You must move from the center of your *ki.*" Or, "Anticipate and maintain proper distance at all times."

I didn't ask the instructor what he meant about my problems with thinking. I merely nodded as if I understood. Wouldn't asking him to clarify mean I was thinking too much? On the other hand, not asking him might have reinforced the notion that I wasn't thinking enough. Of course, just by thinking about this, I was once again thinking too much. You can see why I quit.

*

IN THE MORNING, I use the inn's internet connection to check my emails. My dad's oldest brother emailed me a scan of the genealogy chart I remember seeing years ago. It's not as helpful as I thought it might be— only my grandfather's father and mother are listed and both had question marks by their names and birthdates. There's more information on my grandmother's family in Hawaii, but that won't help me. My uncle tells me his father would clam up when he tried to get him to talk about his family tree.

But it's something.

After breakfast, I take a printout of the chart and go back to the registrar's office. I get a different clerk this time. The one I had yesterday was bored with my request, bored with his job, and he didn't try too hard. Not that I blame him. I couldn't imagine a more tedious job, well, other than editing a technical manual on water towers.

This clerk has a hound-dog face—fat drooping eyelids, fleshy sagging cheeks. He too looks bored but I give him what I know and add the little bit from the genealogy diagram.

He inspects it. "Hard to read," he says. "Can you tell me what it says?"

I go over it with him while he takes notes, writing it out in both Japanese and English. He goes over it a second time with me. When we seem to have it down, he tells me to take a seat and he disappears.

He doesn't come back for nearly an hour. Lugging old, worn books, he motions me up to the counter where he lays out the books. His face is animated, the fleshy cheeks jiggle while he talks.

"The dates are the key. There was a flood in the Taisho Era that destroyed or damaged many records in Katsuyama and Meijiro. I've done some piecing together of what we do have and made some assumptions." He pauses to see if I'm following and understanding.

I nod and he goes on: "Using the dates and the first names of his parents I think we found an entry. We can't be certain, of course, but I think the problem with your grandfather's records is that his name isn't really Hara. It's actually Shimokihara."

"Shimokihara?"

On a piece of paper, he draws the Japanese characters for me and sounds them out. "He must have shortened his name when he arrived in

America. It happened more than occasionally, I hear."

"I didn't know that. Hara is a lot easier. Thank you for finding this out."

"But wait, there's more." He turns to another book. "Shimokihara was only his adopted name."

What? "I've never heard anything about him being adopted."

"That's what the record indicates. Unfortunately, I don't have any way of determining his birth parents. Those records were rarely noted, or if they were, I don't have them."

"So there is absolutely no way to determine his real parents?"

He shakes his head. "Not in this office. But I can tell you typically an adoption occurs in two ways. One would be from one family member to another. His adoptive parents might be his mother's sister, for example. The other would be one family with no sons adopting a male to carry on the family name."

"I see. And you can't tell if any of his adoptive relatives still live in the area?"

"Not that I can see. His adoptive parents had no other children." He looks through the book. "They died around the time you say your grandfather arrived in America."

He gives me a big smile when I thank him and perform a Japanese-style bow. He shakes my hand and says in heavily-accented English, "Nice to meet you." He looks sorry to see me go.

Underlying the *mono no aware* view are the basic beliefs of Shinto—the native religion of Japan. These tenets include:

- nature is beautiful
- nature is harmonious
- nature has intrinsic order and rules
- nature has ethical or moral dimensions

In this philosophy, human nature—what we think, feel, and do—is shaped by the belief that we exist within the order of nature. This belief easily fits into the *mono no aware* experience, which celebrates our emotional responses to objects and events in the natural environment. Unfortunately, few people get away from their urban existence to experience the natural environment.

Fireflies, for example, used to provide families with an excuse to drive to rural wetlands. They gathered in the early evening to watch the display of the glowing insects who live only a few days before their light fades. Now families gather around televisions whose light never fades.

16.

Setsuko Yone acts as professionally as she did yesterday but I sense she is willing to give me time today. I thank her for seeing me and tell her what I'd discovered at the registrar's office. She says, "Your grandfather was adopted and he also changed his name. You were lucky to find out anything at all."

"I agree."

She opens a folder on the table and says, "As you found in the registrar's office, there was a large flood in the Taisho Era. At the time, our town and the town of Katsuyama were actually much closer in population. In fact, Katsuyama was the more well-known village." She shows me copies of old black-and-white photographs. "Here is Katsuyama before the flood. Here it is afterward."

The first photo shows a bustling main street taken from a high vantage point, probably in the hills of the valley. There are crowded two- and three-story buildings, people busy in the streets, hand-drawn carts, piles of boxes next to buildings, a couple of rickety-looking automobiles, electric wires strung crazily. In the second photo, only a couple of buildings remain and they are barely standing. The flood waters smashed or swept away nearly everything, depositing trees and rocks or other debris where buildings once stood.

Setsuko says, "I also found archived newspaper reports and a list of the deceased." She spreads the photocopies on the desk.

We pore over them, me slowly, she quickly. There are reports of deaths, estimated to be over two hundred, most of the village residents were homeless, their crops ruined. Meijiro, built on higher ground for the most part, suffered only minor damage.

"Shimokihara?" Setsuko says suddenly. She points on a list of the dead to my grandfather's adoptive parents.

*

WE GO TO LUNCH at a nice restaurant in a hotel where we look over more of the reports of the flood. She studies each page carefully but quickly, scanning every line. She's become very interested in the story of my grandfather. On the other hand, I take several minutes just to grasp the meaning of a couple of paragraphs and am getting tired of looking at the blurred, small Japanese characters.

"Here!" she says. "Listen to this. A young boy named Shimokihara was interviewed after the flood. He says he was working in his family's fields when the flood hit. His parents were working way across the field, closer to the river. They yelled at him to climb up the slope. He did as he was told and climbed as fast as he could. When he was high enough, he looked down and saw his parents swept away. He says he is still looking for them."

*

I WALK WITH HER back to the museum. I thank her for everything and offer to pay for the copies of the documents. She says it's not necessary; she is happy to have found the information. "It's part of my job."

I say I still owe her something. I offer to take her to dinner that night. She gives me a quick nod, then hands me her card. "Call me after six. My cellphone number is on the back."

She bows and walks into the museum, so suddenly professional again. When she disappears I head for the train station. I get the next train to Katsuyama.

*

THE VILLAGE IS QUIET when I get there, no one in sight. When I walk past the agricultural cooperative, I hear machinery start up. It sounds like a metallic grinder, maybe a blade sharpener. I walk over to the store, make the floorboards on the porch creak, and hear the old woman yell, "Quiet!"

Inside, I nod to her. She says, "Still no Hara around here."

I laugh and she squints at me like I'm a lunatic. "You have a good memory," I say.

"You need another tea?"

"Sure," I say. "I mean please, yes."

We make the transaction. "How about Shimokihara?" I ask her.

"What's that?"

"My grandfather's real family name."

"Shimokihara? No, doesn't ring a bell."

"How about the big flood in 1925? Do you know anything about it?"

Her eyes get wide again. "The flood? I was a little girl then. Only five. But of course I remember it."

I show her the photos from my folder.

She nods at each one. Then I show her the story of the boy named Shimokihara.

She reads it then says, "That's your grandfather, eh? I don't remember him or his parents."

"How about after the flood, do you remember anything about what might have happened to the orphans?"

"No. We moved to another town until they rebuilt Katsuyama. Only a few of us moved back. Only about thirty or forty people."

"Would anyone else here remember the flood?"

She laughs. "I'm the only one left."

I thank her for the information. I walk back down the street toward the fields I'd seen during the first trip. I'm trying to think of a poem. Something that would capture the success of discovering the story of my grandfather's past, of finding some memory of him, if only in a news report. Writing a poem should be easy, there's a lot to work with: a son losing his real parents then watching his adopted parents drown, leaving his devastated village on a ship to a new country where he knew no one, didn't know the language. It should be there.

But I've got nothing.

In experiencing *mono no aware*, the moment must exist without analysis, calmly sinking into the mind so that the significance is felt deeply. Thoughts and feelings become balanced.

Found the thing,
completed the task,
so where's the reward?
Buried deeply ~~and I have no shovel~~
no spade at hand.

17.

IT'S A COUPLE OF weeks into the rainy season when Kumiko returns from Tokyo. The rainy season hasn't been all that rainy but the air hangs dead and muggy. I spend a lot of time in air-conditioning—movie theaters, bookstores, Mos Burger, and especially a quiet coffee shop named Parisian Café where I can sit for hours reading, sketching, writing, or editing for the professor.

Kumiko joins me in the coffee shop. I haven't seen her since she left for Tokyo. I wanted to visit her there, could have used a big city fix—stay at a big hotel with room service and cable, spend days in the Shinjuku Kinokuniya bookstore, eat at Denny's and at all the Mexican restaurants I can find. I miss Mexican food. But Kumiko hadn't invited me to visit and I didn't want to invite myself.

She stirs a sugar cube into her second cup of coffee. "No, it was good. I had a good time."

She says that after telling me she made a lot of tea at her job.

"It was good experience," she goes on. "I got to see what goes on in the publishing business."

"What goes on?" I ask her.

She stares at her dainty spoon. "Lots of meetings. Lots of tea drinking. More meetings."

"Did you get to do any translating?"

She places the spoon on the edge of the saucer, taking great care to balance it just so. "They gave me one trial assignment. It was a short story about a young American girl who saw a kidnapping but no one believes her. I spent many days working on the story. When I turned it in, I thought I'd done a pretty good job. A couple of days later I was called into the head editor's office. He and his two assistant editors were there. They had taken turns making notes on it, each using a different colored pen. Red, blue, green. My translation was covered with red, green, and blue marks.

"The chief editor said that I should study each comment and consider it carefully. He said that the three main problems were my inability to capture the main character's personality, my word choice in translation was too literal and not literary, and that my interpretation of the ending was off."

"Kind of rough," I say.

She nods, sips her coffee.

"Did you redo your translation?"

"I tried to. I read each comment carefully. The weird thing was that often one comment was contradicted by one of the others. Almost like they were arguing among themselves on the page. So in the end, I just gave up on redoing it."

"I'm sorry."

She shrugs. "What about you? Have any flings?"

"Me? Ha." I don't mention Setsuko Yone. It wasn't a fling—we just had dinner. But I do tell Kumiko what I found out about my grandfather.

"Awesome," she says. "What a story. You must be very excited. Have you told your family yet?"

"No. I'm not sure what to say. It's strange that my grandfather wouldn't tell anyone the story. Maybe he didn't want anyone to know. Is there a stigma about adoption here?"

Kumiko thinks for a moment. "It's not very common, I suppose. But I don't think there's a big feeling of shame or anything like that."

"Huh," I say. "Maybe he just didn't want to talk about it."

"Maybe he felt guilty that his parents died and not him."

"Hadn't thought of that. It makes sense. Makes a lot of sense."

*

LATER, THE YAKITORI RESTAURANT on the first floor is at full speed, cranking out its exhaust like an old steam ship. The karaoke machine in the bar is at full volume. We are too tired to make a move out into the world.

Our love-making is listless, as if we are out of practice. I suppose we are. Or else … I asked if she had a boyfriend in Tokyo.

"What?" she says, swatting my arm with a pillow. "Why would you ask that?"

"Just curious."

She doesn't say anything for a while then says, "I was too tired from serving tea all day long to have a boyfriend. I'd just come back to my room and like pass out."

I get the feeling that she did have some sort of experience there, but that it was painful. I know I should leave it alone, but I don't. "Did something happen?"

She flops face down into her pillow. When she doesn't say anything else, I get up, go into the bathroom and shower off. Not so much to get clean, but because the shampoo and soap and water remove the stink of sizzling meat from my nostrils, and the water spraying on me drowns out the karaoke singers.

I'm drying off when I say to Kumiko through the open door to the bathroom, "You remember I once told you about my sort-of girlfriend in L.A."

"Sure. You haven't said anything about her lately."

"I guess not. Well, she's coming to Numazu for a visit. Tomorrow."

"Tomorrow, huh? How long will she be staying?"

"I'm not sure. She didn't say. I suppose she will want to see more of the country, so we might go to Kyoto, too."

"That's good. I'm sure you'll be happy seeing her."

"I know the timing isn't good. You just got back…" That sounds condescending. "I mean, I just found out myself."

"It's okay," she says, but I can hear her dressing. Practically throwing on her clothes.

*

I've been waiting at the Mishima station long before Carine's shinkansen is scheduled to arrive. I had to go to Mishima because there's no bullet train stop in Numazu. Being in Mishima reminds me of the cherry-blossom viewing party. It seems like a lifetime ago.

Pacing along the platform, I realize I'm getting anxious to see Carine. Yes, anxious, rather than excited. I feel like I'm going to make a big fool of myself. Trip over my own feet, slobber on her.

I don't know what our relationship will be like. Not being together, physically, changes a lot of things. It might be better, it might be worse. By worse, I mean not as close as we were. I'm not sure what I mean by better. "Absence makes the heart grow fonder" never made sense to me.

But of course it wouldn't.

I decide there's no way of knowing what it will be like. I'm not sure what to tell her about my experiences here. It's different than I expected. I expected to see the sights for a few weeks and move on. I hadn't expected meeting the professor and hearing about *mono no aware*. I hadn't expected to find out about my grandfather. I hadn't come here for those things. Most of all, I hadn't expected Kumiko.

What I have accomplished here is to push myself into a corner.

It's starting to rain as the train pulls into the station. It glides to a stop; the doors open. I'm looking crazily up and down the platform. Then I see her, and she sees me and smiles and waves. Smiles and waves beautifully. Then she turns to a man standing close to her, too close to be a stranger from the train.

There he is, grinning at me—Joe Creed.

18.

"We met at your going-away party," Carine says after we've settled into the train going to Numazu.

Joe nods at her, then shrugs at me. "What can I say? It was a great party. That reminds me … got a present for you." He digs in his bag.

"You smuggled in a kilo of coffee beans?" I say.

"Better than that," he says. He pulls out something encased in bubble wrap. "A brick of cocaine," he says loudly.

Everyone on the train car strains not to stare at us. The package is heavy, obviously a book. I know what it is before I unwrap it—*Water Tower Design and Field Erection.*

"Fresh off the presses," Joe says.

"Gee, thanks. I can't believe it's already out."

"Had to pull some all nighters," Joe says, glancing at Carine. He opens the book to the title page and points. I've got a mention as one of the editors on the project.

I tell him that I'll cherish it forever.

*

Carine and I are waiting in the lobby of the hotel where she and Joe— Joe!—are staying. Joe is supposedly still getting ready to go out, but I think he wanted to give us some time alone. After an awkward silence she says, "I'm sorry I didn't tell you about Joe."

"No need to apologize. None of my business. Besides I figured something was up. You never mention your love life, so …" I realize I'm setting myself up here.

Carine jumps in with: "You never asked. Plus you never mentioned yours either. So tell me about your love life."

Exactly. "Well … I don't have a love life. I've dated a couple of women. Nothing serious. There is a woman I've dated more than once. She lived in L.A. for a while, teaches at the school where I used to teach. But I told her about you and that you were coming to visit. She was fine with that." Now I'm blathering, dancing on the edge of a lie.

"Good for you," she says.

Though her words might sound sarcastic, Carine is not a sarcastic person. I've never heard her use sarcasm.

I try a little laugh. "It's great to see you. Even with …"

"Look, I'm really surprised it happened. I know you don't like him. But he's a good guy at heart."

"Never said he wasn't. And I never said I didn't like him."

"He speaks highly of you."

"I find that hard to believe."

"No, really. He respects your work as an editor. He said you left the water tower book in great shape. And he's envious of you just picking up and taking off to travel. He said he could never do that."

"It's not that difficult," I say.

"That's not the point … never mind," she says, then turns to me and smiles. "I'm so happy to see you. You look great. Relaxed, I suppose. Gained a little weight."

"I have?"

"Hmm. A little."

"I've been sitting around a lot lately. Guess I need to get out more."

After a pause, she says, "The truck is running well."

"Good. Thanks for taking care of it."

"I hope you don't mind, Joe and I used it once to move some furniture."

"You're living together?"

"No. Well, not really. I got some new furniture."

"No problem," I say. "Use it whenever you want."

*

WE END UP AT the American Bar and Grill where I had my going-away party from the school. We get burgers and beer all around.

Joe says, "I came all the way to Japan and what do I get? A hamburger and a Bud."

"It's the best burger you'll ever have," I say.

"It is very good," Carine says, munching on hers.

"Sure," Joe says. "It's okay. But next time, how about blowfish sashimi? Barbecued eel?"

"I haven't eaten either of those yet since I've lived here," I say. "The fries here are good too."

"Fries. Fries!" Joe groans. "At least some sushi next time. Please."

I raise my hands. "Next meal, I promise. Pure Japanese."

After he washes down a bite of burger with a swig of beer, Joe asks, "So what have you been doing here in … what's the name of this burg again?"

"Numazu," Carine sounds it out correctly.

"I taught at an English conversation school for a while. But I don't have the right visa so I got laid off. I'm doing some editing for a psychology professor. Interesting stuff. The biology of personality."

Joe snorts. "I don't get it. You come all the way to Japan and you're editing research papers and eating burgers and fries? Could've stayed in L.A. to do that."

Carine says, "Tell him about *mono no aware*, Zack."

I forgot I mentioned it once to Carine in an email. "Nah," I say.

Joe says with a glance toward Carine, "What's this?"

Carine says before I can stop her, "Zack's here on a kind of, um, spiritual quest. Looking for a way to experience deep emotions. He heard about a Japanese idea of *mono no aware*, it's … well, you tell him Zack."

"It's not that important," I say.

"Come on," Joe says. "At least it's something interesting."

I swallow a drink of beer while I make something up. "It's not really a quest. It's research. I'm writing a novel based on Japanese aesthetics."

Joe says, "Hara-san! A novel. That's great. Based on Japanese aesthetics.

123

Oh boy. I'm sure it will be a *huge* bestseller. Come on tell me more. What's this *mono* stuff?"

I sigh. "*Mono no aware* is about our emotional reaction to our surroundings or events. Here's an example." I could tell him about the cherry blossoms at Mishima Taisha, but that's my experience with Kumiko. I could tell him about getting lost in Aokigahara, or finding the pear-shaped rock, or the long story about finding out about my grandfather. But those experiences are mine and I don't want to share them, not yet. I'm still trying to figure them out. Instead, I tell him about the suicides at Aokigahara, the tree clinging to the cliff, and how the recent victims ended up cutting their throats.

Carine grimaces and even Joe looks pained as I reach the end of the story. "Geez, Zack," he says, "That's thoroughly unpleasant. If that's what this *mono* stuff is about, then I don't get it at all."

"I'm still trying to figure it out myself."

"Yea, well, good luck with that," Joe says.

*

THEY WANT TO SEE my apartment. We walk up the stairs; the karaoke bar door is open. Joe sticks his head in, and says, "Cool. A real karaoke bar!"

"We can come back after we see Zack's apartment," Carine says.

"At least it's something Japanese," Joe says looking up at me.

I'm already at my apartment door, holding it open. Carine and Joe walk up the last steps and look inside. Joe laughs. "My *suitcase* is bigger than this."

19.

I'M SENDING CARINE AND Joe to the Meijiro hot-springs inn. I let them know that they have seen the highlights of Numazu—the burger joint, my apartment, and the karaoke bar. We did go down there and sing badly but lustily. When I suggested they go to Meijiro, Joe made me swear he will have an authentic Japanese experience. If not, he threatened to tell everyone at Garza I'm eating burgers and drinking Bud and editing scientific articles on my Big Adventure. "You'll never live it down," he said. "I'll make sure of that."

Carine and Joe asked me to go with them to the inn, but I begged off saying I'd just been there and that it was a romantic spot for couples, not for a couple and a third wheel. I don't want to get anywhere near the thought of Carine and Joe being romantic let alone seeing them in action. Carine suggested I bring my friend, and I told her Kumiko is busy.

Joe disappears to go buy some cigarettes, leaving me alone with Carine for only the second time. Carine doesn't have much to say other than it's good to see me and that she misses me. I say I miss her too, miss a lot of things. We don't get any deeper than that. It isn't that I don't have anything deeper to offer. Something is there but it's not explainable in five minutes, maybe not explainable at all.

It feels good to be alone with her. After the initial shock of seeing her with Joe and after the first awkward evening with them, I'm finally getting into being with Carine. Then Joe returns and the train comes and they are gone.

*

LATER THAT DAY, I'M back on the professor's campus with the editing I've completed for him. The rain of the rainy season is finally starting. It's a thick, slow-motion rain and I wish I were headed to the mountains. Maybe that's what I should do, take a vacation. But I'm supposed to be on a vacation already, traveling the world. If I have to go on vacation to get away from my vacation then something isn't working.

When I knock, the professor's door opens slowly. A young woman is holding it open. The professor is at his desk with some papers in front of him. "Sorry," I say, "I didn't know you were with someone. I'm a little early."

"No, please. Come in."

He introduces the young woman as one of his students. She looks at me shyly, even scared. The professor motions for me to take a seat. "I'll just be a minute."

The professor gives feedback on her paper on the psychology of fear. She nods and says, "Yes, yes," at every comment. When he finishes his critique, she leaves and the professor says, "Your friend had a short visit, eh?"

"She went on with her friend to a hot springs then they are going to Kyoto."

"That's too bad you only had a short time to see her."

I don't know what to say, so this comes out: "But that's the way it goes sometimes."

*

WE FINISH GOING OVER the editing, and the professor takes me to dinner at his favorite place for soba. The cold buckwheat noodles and citrusy soy sauce dip are refreshing in the summer heat. We drink beer, sharing large bottles served ice cold. They are quickly coated with condensation from the thick humidity.

"I tried to write a poem but couldn't," I tell him even though he's never asked if I'd completed the assignment. "It's too difficult. I'm not mentally geared for writing a poem."

"Not mentally geared," he repeats. "Your mind has gears?"

"Not a good analogy, I know. Not intellectually capable, not emotionally prepared to write poetry."

"Gears," he says again. This time he smiles then laughs. "I like the idea of gears. I'll use the metaphor sometime. Sorry, what kind of poem are you trying to write?"

"Kind? You mean … ?"

"Short, long, free verse or metered. Japanese style classic haiku or tanka. Are you thinking in English or Japanese?"

"I guess I hadn't really thought about it. I'm using English. I'm trying to capture the essence of a feeling first. I can write about the events, about the scene, but they don't express the emotion. It's not that I can't string some words together resembling a poem." I tell him about the sake-induced poetry contest I had with the inn's proprietor poet.

The professor smiles and repeats my poem about a man full of sake.

"But those aren't poetry with a capital P," I say.

"You have something in mind that you are trying to capture, something those gears are grinding away at?"

I tell him what I found out about my grandfather. "I was in the village where my grandfather grew up with his adopted parents and worked their fields, where he climbed a bank and watched them drown. But I didn't feel a thing."

The professor gazes at his green-brown soba noodles and glistening sauce. With a quick grab and flick of his chopsticks, he dips a thick rope of noodles in the sauce and slurps it up. I watch him chew and swallow the noodles while I drink some beer. When he gets them down, he says, "I think you are trying to do too much at once. You are trying to overcome the inertia of your subconscious and its grip on your emotional life. You have to forget about this first of all. Forget about the events. Forget about your struggle to feel deeply about them. The task wasn't to do everything at once. The task was merely to write a poem.

"Pick a poem that you like or find intriguing. Figure out what you like about it. Then emulate it, substituting what you discovered about your grandfather. Don't worry about the emotion, it will come."

I nod and refill our beer glasses.

*

ALONG WITH THE REASSIGNED poetry task, he assigns me another: "You expressed some interest in the people who commit suicide together in one of these so-called suicide clubs. Your task is to discover why these people decided to end their lives. Use your art and poetry to convey their decisions."

"That sounds very difficult," I say.

He nods, slurps soba.

Slurping soba, singing songs.
Tippling tea, thinking things.
A night on the town
not much else.

20.

"YOUR FRIEND LEFT? ALREADY?" Kumiko says.

I waited for her outside the school. "She went with her friend to the Meijiro hot-springs inn. After that they're going to Kyoto."

"Without you?" she says.

"Hard to believe, isn't it?"

She shakes her head. "I suppose it's not so hard to believe. Not if she has a new friend."

"What are you doing now?"

"Right now? I have plans. Lots of old boyfriends have called me up lately and I don't know which one to see first. It's such a problem."

"Good for you."

"But I can call them and let them know something has come up."

"You would?"

"If you're nice to me."

"I promise."

She grabs my arm and pulls me away. "We better get away from the school."

"In case one of your old boyfriends sees us together?"

"In case the police come back."

"Are they still looking for illegal teachers?"

"They were talking with the director again."

We go to my favorite coffee shop and get coffee and cake. The bright lights of the shop are garish, the spotless surfaces magnifying the effect.

She asks, "Did your friend have a good time in Numazu?"

"I don't think so. It was kind of uncomfortable."

She nods. "My L.A. boyfriend visited Japan once. It wasn't very good either. He didn't like Japan so much. He was nervous the whole time."

"I think Carine likes Japan."

"It was uncomfortable because she came with her new friend."

I nod, sip coffee.

"Her new friend is more than a friend."

"Yes."

"Oh," she says. "I'm sorry."

I shake my head. "It's nothing to be sorry about. She's her own person. It's just that her new friend, Joe, is someone I know. Someone who ..."

"He's a rival?"

"No, not a rival." I smile at the thought.

"Someone you don't like?"

That's closer. "I actually like the guy in a weird way. He's just, well, not someone I expected her to go out with."

"I see. Now it's Carine and Joe, and you don't feel too happy about it because you don't understand it."

"I guess that's right." Then I suddenly laugh, unexpectedly finding the whole situation absurd. "I just hope he doesn't drive my truck again."

She gives me a questioning look.

"Never mind," I say.

*

WE ARE ON OUR second cup of coffee and second piece of cake. I'm sure Joe would appreciate another slice of modern Japan—coffee and cake.

"I'm thinking of going away for a few days," I tell Kumiko. "I'm doing some research."

"What kind of research? Where are you going?"

"I'm not sure where yet. I'm going to try to find out something about these four people." I pull out a folder from my backpack and show her the newspaper clipping I found in the L.A. airport.

She reads it. "Aokigahara again?"

"It's tied into the *mono no aware* research I'm doing. The professor recommended I find out why they killed themselves."

She looks skeptical. "I don't understand what that has to do with *mono no aware*. I thought the term is used in literary analysis."

"I'm not sure if there is the connection between the suicide victims and *mono no aware*. The professor doesn't tell me the purpose of the tasks until after I complete them."

She pushes cake crumbs between the tines of her fork. "You need to do this research by yourself?"

"What do you mean?"

"I mean … I'm kind of feeling like I don't want to be alone right now."

"No, I don't have to do it alone. Actually, I'd rather not do it alone. Do you want to help?"

"If I can be of help."

"I don't know how easy or difficult it will be to find where these people lived, find their families and friends. And if we find them, I don't know if they will want to talk to us." I give her a smile. "I would love your help."

"Great! I know a news reporter who might have information."

"Perfect. You're helping already."

"Helping you find out their stories might help me too."

"Help you too?"

"Help me translate fiction. I might understand endings better."

*

WE END THE EVENING with a soak in my tub in my apartment no bigger than Joe's suitcase. She feels good squashed against me. I thought it would be Carine with me this night. Kumiko is probably thinking that I'm thinking it should be Carine squashed against me.

"Did you tell her about me?" Kumiko asks.

"I did."

"You told her you have a Japanese girlfriend?"

Not exactly, but I say, "Yes." I reach down to her abdomen and she shivers. She turns and faces me, guides me into her, and closes her eyes while we create tsunami waves in the tiny tub.

Genji describes *mono no aware* in its many forms and makes the reader conscious of the emotions and expressions offered in the stories. Norinaga claimed that there is no significance in novels and poems apart from *mono no aware*. His theory of literature contrasts with the then prevailing view of literature as a piece of moral instruction, usually based on Confucian and Buddhist concepts of "good and evil." Norinaga's concepts of good and evil, as applied to literature, derive from whether the work is in harmony with the deepest feelings of men and women.

Love moves people deeply and so it is an especially rich source for the *mono no aware* experience. An illicit love affair creates a particularly strong feeling of *mono no aware* because its public expression has to be suppressed. The story of *Genji* has many love affairs, including illicit ones, not in order to merely induce sensuality but to illustrate the *mono no aware* deeply involved in love and sensuality. Norinaga likens one who appreciates the *mono no aware* involved in illicit love affairs to the man who "stores muddy water in order to plant a lotus and appreciate lotus flowers." Illicit love affairs, while not in line with the morals of the time (at least explicitly), were appreciated for the deep emotions they aroused, especially because they had to be kept secret.

21.

KUMIKO LEFT A NOTE next to the futon: "Need to take care of a few things. Meet you back at the coffee shop at 11."

I'm feeling lethargic, weighed down. It could be from a lack of sleep—too much coffee and cake. It might be the rainy season's muggy blanket. I crank up the air, not so much for the cool but to suck out the dampness in the air. In a few minutes I'm feeling better. I check the time: it's only a little after nine, so I settle back in my futon.

This morning I'm not quite as sure about the task of finding out about the suicide victims as I was yesterday. Finding out why they killed themselves seems impossible. Can't ask them, that's for sure. Maybe they left notes or told family or friends their motives. But I am curious. And who knows, I might be able to write a poem or two about what we find. Although uncovering my grandfather's story didn't help much with my poetry. So far, this is all I can come up with:

> *Pulling weeds, ending their lives,*
> *my name floats on the dark clouds*
> *and then running, higher, I watch the water*
> *sweep them away.*

A technical writer's first attempt at poetry.

I try a few more, then sigh and toss aside the notebook. I grab a quick shower and get dressed and head for the coffee shop. Nothing like the hair of the dog.

*

Kumiko greets me with a smile and an enthusiastic "good morning!"

She folds her legs under the table, places a short stack of papers on the table.

"Good morning," I say. "You look happy today."

"I do? I'm always happy, aren't I?"

I smile, not disagreeing. She orders her coffee.

"You left early," I say.

"Not that early, sleepyhead. I went to visit my reporter friend." She pats the papers. "This is a copy of a news agency's reporting and research on the suicide. There's also a list of the victims from a police report with their ages, occupations, and home towns. Also, they had printed pages from the suicide website where the victims met."

"You're wonderful." I skim through the information.

"He said he'll try to find other information if he can."

"He's being very helpful. Please thank him for me. Did you have to promise him anything to get the information?"

Kumiko laughs. "You mean like a date? No. The only thing he asked was to let him know if we find anything he might be interested in for a follow-up story. Now what should we do?"

I show her the list of names. "We should start with the leader of the group." Attorney Fumio Murano, resident of Yokohama, was thirty-two when he died. He placed the initial advertisement on the suicide website, not using his real name of course. His suicide-pseudonym was "Sailor."

*

Kumiko and I take the train to Yokohama, about two hours from Numazu. It feels good sitting on the sleek train, sitting next to her, watching the seaside and countryside skim past. We don't say much but it's okay just being together.

We check into a cheap business hotel near the station. Our room is functional, sterile, in high contrast to the serene expansiveness of the hot-springs inn at Meijiro. We drop off our bags in the room, then go out to meet the reporter at the local newspaper whom Kumiko's friend called before we left Numazu.

The streets are crowded with cars, trucks, buses, taxis. We're in one of the latter, splurging but also needing to get to the newspaper in time for the meeting. I sit back and watch the scurrying. It's good to be in a big city for a couple of days. Yokohama reminds me of downtown L.A.—sleek, busy, and vertical.

Kumiko dressed up for the day, wearing one of her Tokyo work outfits. I dug up one of the professional shirts and ties I put away after I lost my job at the school. She is looking out the window of the taxi, thinking about something. I have no idea about what. Really, I can't guess. I realize I don't know much about her. She maintains a firewall against intrusion into her most intimate thoughts.

As the taxi pulls up to a high-rise office building, I'm feeling like this isn't going to get us anywhere. It's a wild goose chase. I doubt a big city reporter will want to help two unknown people with vague motives and a many-months-old story.

In the lobby we find the floor to go to and take the elevator. It's a glass-enclosed car, giving riders a view of the building's open atrium. Kumiko and I stand in the very back of the crowded car, so we don't get much of a view. The two of us are pressed together and that feels good, so who cares about the view.

The floor where we get out is busy—the newspaper employees are on the run or if not running, at least in the smooth, rapid pace of a race walker. All conversations are in clipped phrases: "I'll call." "Can't today." "No way."

It takes several minutes to find the reporter. He's got longish, frazzled hair, like he's been standing out in the wind. He greets us warmly, telling us he was glad to hear from his old journalism school friend in Numazu.

He motions us to a nearby conference room. "So you are doing research on the suicide club, is that right?"

I answer: "I'm working for Professor Imai at Numazu University. He's writing an article on personality traits."

"You're American?" he asks. "Japanese American?"

"Yes," I say.

"Your Japanese is very good," he says.

I give the standard denial in deference to modesty.

The reporter says, "I've written a few articles on the phenomenon." He pushes a folder across his desk. "You can have these copies."

Kumiko and I glance through them. They report facts about the suicide clubs and their websites. They lay out suicide trends and statistics and the effects on families and society in general.

"These will be very helpful," I say. "We also want to look at some specific cases."

"Case studies," the reporter says and nods.

"In particular, do you have any information about this one." I show him the articles Kumiko found in Numazu. "One of the victims is from Yokohama. Fumio Murano."

The reporter claps his hands together. "Murano. Yes, of course, a very interesting case."

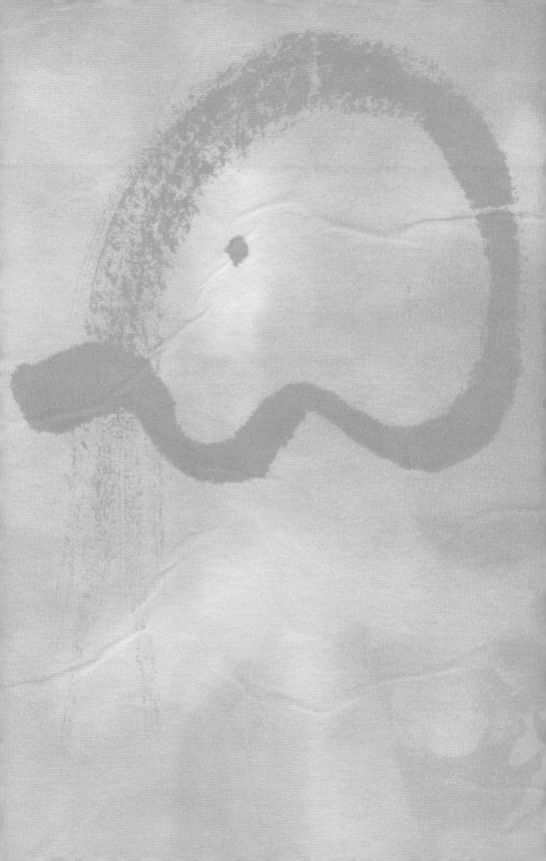

22.

By the time we get out of the reporter's office, it's getting late. We tried to get the reporter to go with us to dinner, but he shook his frazzled head of hair and said, "Deadline." We take our riches of information on suicide clubs and the attorney to Yokohama's Chinatown. After walking around for a few minutes checking out window displays, we settle into a small restaurant off the main street.

We order food and drink then each take half of the papers. While we read, we tell each other interesting tidbits we find.

"…graduated first in his class…

…one of the youngest ever hired…

…top-rated amateur sailboat racer…

…hired by a prestigious law firm in their international corporate division…

…rising star…

…one of Yokohama's most eligible bachelors."

We pause to eat Chinese, share a beer. After downing a shrimp, I say, "Seems like he had every reason to live."

"Maybe too many reasons," Kumiko says. "Too many expectations. Life could never be fully satisfying for him. He lost himself in all his accomplishments. But we will never know for sure, will we?"

"Did it say anywhere if he left a suicide note?"

We look through the papers related to the suicide. Nothing is mentioned about a note.

"What about this sailing accident?" Kumiko points to a couple of paragraphs in one of the reports.

A year before his suicide, Murano and a school friend were sailing Murano's small sailboat off the coast in a rural area. As they were hauling in the boat, the mast hit a power line. The electric shock killed his best friend. Murano wasn't touching the boat at the time and wasn't injured. He tried to revive his friend until a rescue vehicle arrived in fifteen minutes but too late to do any good.

Kumiko says, "Do you think it has anything to do with his suicide?"

"It might. We need to talk with someone close to him."

"If we can find anyone."

*

IN THE MORNING, WE follow the leads on Murano's past life to a sister living in Yokohama. She was skeptical at first about meeting us. I can hardly blame her. We have the thinnest of credentials.

On the way to her apartment, we pass the port and harbor, lined with skyscrapers. It's been a harbor for hundreds of years. I read that bit of trivia in one of the tourist brochures at the hotel. The port is probably where my grandfather caught the ship that took him to Hawaii.

"Beautiful," Kumiko says, reading my mind.

The taxi slows after a few minutes in a neighborhood of condominium high-rise buildings. The taxi lets us out and we find the number of her unit and press the intercom button. She answers right away, and we are buzzed into the building.

The lobby has marble sculpture, gold light fixtures, paintings, a flower arrangement on a glass table. We take the elevator up to her floor. Soft classical music is playing for our enjoyment. We find our host's condo and ring the bell. The door opens immediately.

Murano's sister is maybe thirty-five. Kumiko and I go through our formal bowing and introduction and apology routine. Satisfied, she lets us in and we sit in a Western-style living room on long sofas positioned with a view toward the sea. She asks if we would like something to drink, and we say don't go to any trouble. She smiles and disappears for a moment. She brings out bottled water in individual ice buckets and crystal glasses.

She is wearing a very fashionable yet casual outfit: a form-fitting turtleneck and pants of silk or a silky fabric. She wears designer glasses and gold earrings. I feel underdressed in my jeans and polo shirt. Kumiko is much better off in her skirt and silk blouse. The sister pours our water. The label says it's purified deep sea water from Hawaii. Probably twenty dollars a bottle.

"So you knew my brother," she says.

She's got it all wrong already. "Ah, sorry. We didn't know him personally. Only about him. We are compiling psychological case studies and your brother was recommended to us during the course of our research."

She nods listlessly and glances at our water which we haven't touched. As if on cue, we take a sip to appease her.

It tastes like water. "Yummy," I say.

"Sorry to be so direct," Kumiko says, "but we would like to hear your impressions of your brother. In particular we would be interested to know your thoughts on why he committed suicide."

I'm glad Kumiko is taking over. We look at the sister sympathetically and expectantly.

She exhales a little breath of air. "Of course it was his girlfriend's fault. She wanted to marry him. Obsessed with it. He wanted to focus on his work first. That makes sense, doesn't it? He is only … wasn't even thirty yet."

Kumiko asks, "Had they been going together for a long time?"

She glances up at the ceiling. It's a high ceiling. "Three, no four years. Is that long?"

I say, "Not too long, but not too short either."

She looks satisfied with my answer.

Kumiko asks, "Still it seems unlikely that he would have killed himself over her insistence."

The sister blinks behind her glasses. "Really? I thought you said you knew my brother. He was always trying to please people. Please *everyone*. He hated it when he couldn't give people the answer they wanted to hear."

"It must be hard to do that," I say. "Especially when you are an attorney. I imagine you have to give people bad news all the time."

"Exactly!" says the sister, slapping one hand onto the palm of the other.

Kumiko says, "What about the sailing accident? That must have been horrible for him."

The sister tops off our glasses of desalinated, deep-sea water. "Funny thing though, he never wanted to talk about it. He didn't go to his friend's funeral. I went on his behalf. He said he didn't think it appropriate that he go."

"Did he seem different after the funeral?"

"I didn't see him much after that. He was always busy with work. And his girlfriend … she kept him close to her."

"So the suicide was a real shock," Kumiko says.

She closes her eyes, grimaces. When she opens them she says, "It was her fault." She emphasizes each word equally.

"The girlfriend?" I ask just to clarify.

The sister lifts her glass, her hand shaking. Not much, but enough to see.

23.

THE EVENING IS MUGGY, steamy. To be precise, it's still 32°C with 80 percent H. Real feel: miserable. I'm meeting the professor at Mama-san's bar. When I walk in, the bar's cool, dry interior hits me right away and wipes away the first sheen of perspiration. Mama-san greets me more with a friendly, familiar note to her voice. The professor is already perched on his favorite stool. He gives me a welcoming nod and already has a drink poured for me when I sit down. The whisky-water with lots of ice looks good tonight. Nice and cold.

After a cooling sip, I ask how he is doing.

"Good. I've finished reading my students' final papers."

"Congratulations," I say and raise my glass. His cheeks are a little flushed.

He says, "I would like to finish up the paper edits in the next few days."

I tell him I have time. Kumiko and I just returned from Yokohama. We didn't have any more luck with Murano's case. The sister didn't know anything about the suicide club. She gave us the name of the supposedly demanding girlfriend but we couldn't track her down. No one at the law firm where Murano worked would talk to us. Neither would any of the family of Murano's friend killed in the sailing accident. We came back from Yokohama after two and a half days.

The professor and I plan when we will work on the edits. I'm feeling better, cooled and warmed at the same time. When we've set a schedule, I tell him what Kumiko and I found out about Murano. "I'm not sure that the sailing accident was the cause of his suicide. It happened a full year before he killed himself. Yes, the sister did raise the point that he wanted to please everyone so it must have been a big blow when he was responsible, even indirectly, for his friend's death." I pause, gazing at the professor, who is focused on the ice in his glass. Then I catch him stealing a glance at his watch.

I go on, "The sister's belief that the girlfriend's demands were responsible might have merit, but I just don't see it. Still, the sister was adamant that was the cause."

The professor sucks in a breath and shakes his head. "It's difficult to say, isn't it? What do you think? I mean what do you think he felt?"

I'm not sure. Kumiko suspects the accident, the death of his friend, was the root cause of his suicide. I shake my head and shrug at the same time. "He lived such a different life from mine. I can't imagine how he felt."

"It's interesting he chose to lead a suicide group. Your description of his personality reminds me of someone who would be ashamed of committing suicide. Someone who tries to please everyone and ultimately fails. I imagine him hiking far out into the woods to kill himself. But what did he say? 'Dying alone is lonely?'"

"Does that imply he was afraid to be by himself? He might have lacked the courage to commit suicide on his own. But with others he could."

"Possibly, although that still doesn't answer the main question of why."

No it doesn't. "I'll have to do more research."

We drink and eat, chat with Mama-san. I get up the courage to show him some of my poems. I'd worked on them some more, thinking about Johei's poetry. I figure if the accountant/proprietor can do it, so can I.

The professor reads a few. One is about a garden seen through an old, elaborate gate. The other is about ecstasy, rain, and not caring. He glances away from the page—at his watch—then reads them again.

"That bad?" I say.

"No. It's … they are not bad attempts."

"Not good either."

"Their quality isn't the point. The object of the task was to write a poem. And you've done that."

"I would prefer to write good poems."

"Poetry is not something that pops into your head. It's a skill as much as insight, practice as much as talent. Of course, you know that."

"So it's not the same then as *mono no aware*. It's not an innate

152

personality trait."

"I would agree with that for the most part. One is needed for the other, however."

"*Mono no aware* is needed for the poet; poetry is needed for *mono no aware*?"

"To fully experience *mono no aware*, poetic abilities are needed. To have both fully formed, one requires the other."

"That's why you want me to write poetry."

He nods.

*

WE LEAVE THE BAR early, the professor saying he has to go back to the university. I walk out of the bar with him toward the station. When we come to my apartment building, we say good-bye and he hurries away. I start to walk up the stairs when I realize I need a beer or two to get through the night. I go back down and head toward the vending machines at the corner liquor store. I'm about there when I see the professor walking past the station. I wonder if he wanted to just get rid of me.

For whatever reason, I'm really not sure why, I start to follow him. The streets are crowded enough so that I can follow him discretely. I feel a little guilty about following him, he's entitled to his personal life. I wonder if he's backtracking to return to Mama-san's bar so he can be there without me. He could be having an affair with her. They seem to have a relationship beyond bar owner and customer. I wonder if an affair with her was responsible for the professor's divorce.

He walks to the end of the block then turns down a street. I hurry ahead and get to the street and stop. I see him walking ahead, more quickly now, as if he's late for an appointment. There's no one else on the street, making it difficult for me to keep from being discovered, so I just watch him.

When he turns down a narrow alleyway, I run ahead. I stop at the alley and peer around a building. About halfway down the alley, he walks inside a building. I wait a couple of minutes then go down the alley. The building he entered is a doctor's office.

No anger, no pain.
No joy, no ecstasy.
So what? Who cares?
It rained today.

Motoori Norinaga observed that the ability to discern joy or sadness while experiencing the world depended on the person and the context. Some people are highly tuned and they find the emotive essence in nearly everything and can "sing" about the *mono no aware* they encounter. Others have no discernment and they have no song in their heart. The vast majority lie between these two extremes, capable of seeing *mono no aware*, but only rarely and in narrow situations.

24.

CLOUDS HANG OVERHEAD BUT hold onto their load of rain. Only a couple more weeks of the rainy season. At least that's what they say.

I meet Kumiko in the coffee shop, a cup of coffee on the table in front of her. We haven't seen each other for a few days. She told me she's been busy with teaching and work. I've been editing for the professor. With the rest of my time, I read and write and sketch. Watch bad TV.

"I'm okay," she answers when I ask how she's doing. "Maybe a little tired."

She does look tired. But the rainy season makes everyone look tired. "Are you still busy?"

"Crazy busy. Or just crazy. Did your friends come back to visit?"

"No. They stayed in Kyoto for a few days, then went back to Tokyo without stopping in Numazu. They are staying there for two days then going home."

"Didn't you want to go to Tokyo to see them?" she asks.

"Not really. I mean, I'd feel strange."

She sips her coffee. "Are we going to look for the next person on the list?"

"If you want to help me, that would be great. If you're too busy then that's okay."

She shakes her head. "I have two days off. So let's go!"

*

DAISUKE KUDO, TWENTY-ONE WHEN he died, lived in a suburb of Tokyo, one of the satellite communities popping out from Tokyo central like sprouting mushrooms. We are going to have a more difficult time finding out about him than we did about the attorney Murano who had a more public life. Our only information on Kudo is the name and town where he lived.

The suburb town is a bullet-train ride from Numazu, then a train ride to a transfer, then another local train trip. We left before dawn and I sleep through more than half of the train ride. Kumiko falls asleep on my shoulder and that feels good.

She's not too talkative when we are awake at the same time. But she does tell me that she's applying for another job in publishing in Tokyo. "I hope it goes better this time. I've been practicing translating fiction. Could you help me when you get a chance?"

"I'd be happy to."

The local train arrives at our destination. We get out and drift with the flow of departing passengers. The area immediately around the station is occupied by department stores and a pedestrian mall squeezed between them. Kumiko and I look at each other, not sure what to do first.

"I'm hungry," she says.

We wander down the pedestrian mall and find a restaurant among the many there. We both order curry-rice—mine beef, hers chicken.

"What's the plan?" Kumiko asks.

I don't know. We did some research before we left Numazu but didn't find anything from a web search or calls to the local papers. There was no phone number for him in the old listing we found. Apparently, he wasn't born in the suburb because he wasn't in the local registrar's office.

"Do you have any ideas?"

"How about the police?" Kumiko says.

"You mean maybe he has a criminal record?"

"The local police keep records of neighborhood inhabitants."

"Good idea."

Our curry-rice arrives. Kumiko's looks better than mine.

*

IT TAKES US FIVE police substations and all afternoon to find a record of Daisuke Kudo. We follow the police officer's directions to a row of four-story buildings — businesses on the ground floors, apartments above. The building where Kudo lived has a business supply store on the first floor.

We climb the stairs of the building and find his apartment on the second floor. Of course, there's a new name in the resident's plate next to the door. I ring the bell. Maybe the person knows something about Kudo.

I ring the bell again. No one answers. There are three other apartments on the floor. We split up, ring bells. No one is home, or if they are, they aren't answering.

"How about the store downstairs?" Kumiko says.

We go back down the stairs and then inside the store. They stock paper, ink cartridges, a huge collection of pens and pencils, day planners, some small electronics. There's a row of copy machines.

We find an employee to talk to—a young woman, her hair dyed a reddish-blonde. She is ringing up sales for a man wearing a business suit and an unlit cigarette between his fingers. He fidgets with the cigarette and when he gets his change, he hurries out of the store.

While I'm admiring a display of high-tech, colorful pens and mechanical pencils, Kumiko goes over to the clerk and asks about Kudo. The clerk gives her a vacant look at first then claps her hands together. "Oh, you mean Slipper!" she says.

Metaphor, in literary terminology, is a word or phrase which in standard or literal usage denotes one kind of thing, quality, or action applied to another, in the form of a statement of identity instead of comparison ("my brother is a saint"). The Japanese poets particularly used nature in implicit metaphors, that is, the meaning is implied by the verbal context. When the poet wrote about cicadas singing only at dusk, it likely referred to unrequited love.

25.

THE BUSINESS SUPPLY STORE clerk, Chiyako, told us to meet her after work at a statue of a lion near the entrance to the pedestrian mall. Apparently it's a popular place to arrange a meeting because twenty or thirty people are waiting near the lion, their eyes searching the crowd for a familiar face. When their target is spotted, they relax and wave or, if young girls, give a little squeal.

Chiyako didn't give us much information at the store as it suddenly got very busy with customers. Other than where to meet her, the only thing she had time to tell us was that Slipper was Daisuke Kudo's nickname. She looked sad when she told us.

Kumiko and I only have to wait a few minutes for her to show up. We wave but don't squeal. She clomps over to us in thick-soled shoes. Without her clerk's apron, she looks younger. She takes us to a pub when we ask her to pick a spot for us.

The pub is crowded, but we find a table in the back. I go get us drinks and something to munch on. I'm gone several minutes and when I get back with beer and fried mushrooms, Kumiko and Chiyako are deep in conversation.

Kumiko tells me: "Kudo's nickname was Slipper because he used to wear only flip-flops."

"He was a real creature of habit," Chiyako says.

"Even in the winter?"

OH!

Chiyako nods. "He would wear the same pair until they fell apart. Somebody asked him once why he wore them and he said, 'They're comfortable.'"

"How did you meet him?" I ask.

Kumiko says, "He was an artist so he was always coming down from his apartment to get supplies. Right?" Kumiko looks at Chiyako.

She nods. "He never had much money so I'd give him credit. Of course, I ended up paying his bill half the time. I think almost everything he earned at his job went to his rent. He was always hungry." As if she is hungry too, she picks up a mushroom and pops it in her mouth.

"What did he do for a living?" I ask.

"He worked part-time at a night shift at a factory making packaged foods for convenience stores. I know he had to wear a hair net and gloves because he sometimes brought home used ones. I'm not sure what he did with them."

"What kind of drawing did he do?" Kumiko asks.

"Anime, manga. He didn't talk about it much. He showed me a few things that he'd drawn. They were pretty good, at least I thought they were."

I ask, "Did he try to get a job as an artist?"

Chiyako says, "One time I told him that he should get a job in the anime or manga business. He said that he wasn't nearly good enough. And he said he was way too slow. It took him weeks and several attempts just to do one of his drawings. At least that's what he said."

"You didn't believe him?" Kumiko asks.

Chiyako thinks for a moment. "He was very good, in my opinion. And it seemed that he had a lot of drawings for someone who took weeks to do one." She pauses, turns her beer glass on the coaster a half turn, then another half turn. "He seemed to be happy just that I'd look at his art and say it was good."

Kumiko asks, "Were you and he good friends?"

Chiyako smiles. "I know what you mean. No, we weren't involved at all. I have a boyfriend. Slipper and I only saw each other when I was at work. Well, that's not true. A couple of times we ran into each other at the store or the train station."

164

"Do you think he wanted more?" Kumiko asks. "More of a relationship?"

She shakes her head and frowns. Then she nods once, twice. "I think he was too shy to ask me out though."

"Was there anything else you can tell us about him?" I ask.

Chiyako tilts her head. "Anything else?"

"Did he seem like someone who would commit suicide?"

"Not at all. But I don't know anyone who has, so it's hard for me to imagine. I was really shocked when I heard about it. He didn't seem depressed, if that's what you mean. He never talked about suicide."

"What happened to all of his drawings?" I ask.

"I don't know where they went. The police came one day right after the suicide, boxed everything, and took it away. They probably sent it to his parents."

"Do you know where they are?"

"I don't know anything about his family. He never mentioned them."

"What about his drawings? What were they about?" Kumiko asks.

Chiyako taps her finger on the glass. "Nothing dark. Nothing about suicide or dying. They were usually of kids, boys or girls, walking through fantasy landscapes. You know, with high mountains, or deep forests. He liked water too. Waterfalls, lakes."

She looks away and says quietly, "Now that I think about it, he might have been drawing him and me in one of his imagined worlds."

*

WE ARE WALKING BACK through the mall toward the train station. "Did you know he was involved in a suicide club?" I ask.

She looks pained at this question. "Like I said, he never mentioned suicide, never talked about a club. But I can see him getting involved in one. He probably would have liked being around the others in the club. Just to be around them, if you know what I mean."

Another guiding principle of *mono no aware*
is the idea that these aesthetic moments lie
suspended, in space and time, between the
observer and the observed. This distance
represents our mental and emotional existence
in the world, a zone where we interact with
our environment. This space does not support
our human narcissism, rather it introduces us
to a different point of view. The space allows
us to step out of our mental life and examine
ourselves in comparison to a slice of the
universe as it really is. This space is not so
much about values such as beauty or ugliness
as it is about the essence of being, which
cannot be easily described or categorized.

26.

I'M WAITING OUTSIDE THE train station for the professor. We are going to go over the last few pages of editing. I'm looking forward to finishing the project but at the same time it will be the end of my employment.

He arrives and nods at me in greeting. "Are you hungry?" he asks.

"I could eat," I say.

"I could eat," the professor repeats.

"That phrase has always puzzled me. Could is a conditional. Could eat *if* something happens. Could eat if food were put in front of me. So it implies a slight hunger."

I nod and the professor grins as if discovering a great truth. "Let's walk a little to build up your appetite."

"Sure," I say, happy the day's English lesson is over.

We head toward the ocean along the side streets of Numazu. The professor asks how I'm progressing on my latest task.

"It's been difficult," I say. "We found only a little information about two of the four suicide victims." I tell him what we learned about Slipper. "The problem is understanding the victim's motives from people's impressions of the victim's motives. I'm not sure it's possible to grasp the motives, the emotional content, of their reason for suicide."

The professor says, "It requires imagination to assume what others are feeling. Is that what you mean?"

I nod. "Even if I could imagine what it would be like in their situation,

I would probably be wrong. I doubt if I could fully grasp their emotional life."

"That's true. We can't be certain. Even if that person told us what he was experiencing, we can only try to understand the feeling from our own experiences. Comparing it to a similar situation. Similar but never the same."

Sure, that makes sense. But I'm hardly in a position to draw upon similar situations. "It makes the task of writing a poem about the victims even more difficult. I can write about the circumstances of their lives, what people have told me, about their lives. But that doesn't make a poem, does it?"

The professor murmurs agreement.

We walk along the beach for a while. Not a sandy beach, it's covered with wave-polished stones and pebbles. A few shore fishermen, sitting on folding chairs, tend their poles. Along the banks of the river flowing through Numazu are massive tetrahedral-shaped concrete blocks, twice as tall as I am, deposited to protect the banks and seawall from erosion. Only technical writers and engineers could find the manmade monstrosities of any interest, so I find the sight fascinating. I imagine a huge alien being playing with its jacks.

We head back toward town. "Could you eat now?" the professor asks.

"I'm starving," I say.

The professor laughs. "So now you *must* eat."

*

WE ARE WALKING DOWN a narrow side street for a few blocks when I realize it's the same street as the doctor's office. Before we reach it, he stops at an unassuming building, the front covered in old, worn cedar planks. The windows are covered with paper screens. There is no sign on the building.

Inside, shoes clutter the entryway, which is cobbled with beach stones. There is a warm smell of food and then a muffled burst of laughter from somewhere deep inside the restaurant. When we step onto a slightly raised platform, a kimono-clad woman bustles over and greets the professor by name. I'm introduced and we are shown to a private room with soft tatami mats and a low table. "It's an old house," the professor tells me. "An artist and poet lived here until he died thirty or so years ago. His family turned it into this restaurant. Invitation only!"

"I'm impressed."

"No menu. They only serve what they get fresh. It's the best food around."

*

AND IT IS. WE'VE reviewed only about half of the editing when we are served our first course: horse-mackerel sashimi. We're drinking sake, as good as I've had, even better than the "rough local" sake at the Meijiro hot-springs inn. We give up doing any more work and enjoy the meal. Our conversation drifts from one topic to the next.

When we've finished, we walk back toward the train station. We pass the doctor's office. I check the professor out of the corner of my eye to see if he acknowledges it. He doesn't, not that I notice anyway.

We get to the train station. I thank him for the great meal. He waves it off, goes into the station while I head for my apartment. At the corner, I hide behind a wall and peer around it. After a moment the professor pops out of the train station.

I follow him to the side street. I stop at the corner and watch him go inside the doctor's office. I hurry down the street to the building. It looks closed, dark and empty. I walk past the entry a couple of times. As I'm about to go up to the door, a woman turns toward the building. She sees me and gives me a questioning look.

"Is it open?" I ask her.

"No. It's closed," she says. "Try the clinic on the other side of the station."

I thank her and walk away. At the corner I turn and watch. After a few minutes, no one else has gone into the building. I walk back toward it, but this time I go right in.

The reception room is dark except for the reflected light coming from a hallway. I go down the hallway and hear voices. Near the end of the hallway is an open door; the voices come from the room behind the door. I duck into one of the exam rooms and listen.

When my breathing slows, I hear a few voices from inside the clinic. I can make out maybe two women, maybe three or four men. They are discussing nothing about a patient, or diagnosis, or treatment. Instead, they discuss which word or phrase might be better, or disagree about a traditional form of poetry. One of the men delivers a lengthy soliloquy about capturing the meaning of a rustling bamboo grove.

Then I hear the professor's voice: "… for it to succeed you must more deeply understand the *mono no aware* of the moment, the very instant when you perceive your true feelings. Without that understanding, your poem about death can only fail. It's at the moment of death when we should experience the height of *mono no aware*."

Motoori Norinaga goes even further by stating that those who do not experience *mono no aware* have no soul, no heart. "Soul" and "heart" (*kokoro*) refer to our affective or emotional being. Of course, we are all born with the biology of emotions built into our nervous systems. However, Norinaga seems to be stating that we do not all have the ability to tap into, to use, these emotions. Having a "heart" means being able to discern the essence of a moment of joy, love, or sadness. But is a "heart" the result of biology (some may be more endowed than others) or training (learning to use the emotional part of the nervous system)? In other words, is a "heart" due to nature or nurture?

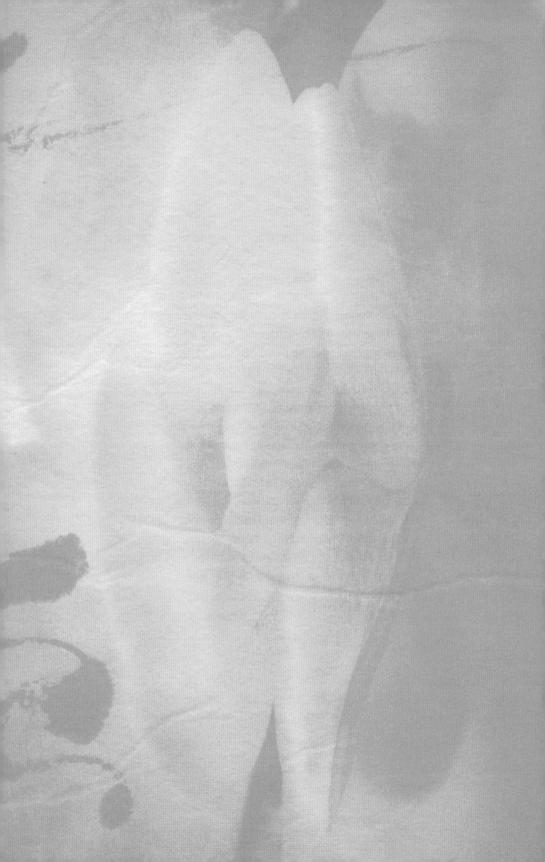

27

KUMIKO AND I ARE on the far northern side of Tokyo in a semi-industrial area. After an all-day train trip from Numazu we checked into a cheap hotel just off a highway. We flopped onto the bed in the spare, tiny room and haven't moved since.

Hiromi Yamazaki brings us here. Twenty-three years old when he joined the other three in the car parked at Aokigahara, his distinguishing feature was a heavily tattooed torso. We have photos of his tattoos. That's all we know about him.

On the nightstand next to me is a can of beer and a cellophane package of dried horse mackerel—the latter a gift from the professor. While drinking and chewing, I'm reading the short story Kumiko wants to translate for practice. The story from *The New Yorker* is about a college student, originally from India though he has lived in America with his father and mother for many years. His mother died recently and his father has already remarried. The father went back to India to find a new wife, and he returned with the woman and her two young daughters, one aged seven and one ten.

The student comes home for the holidays to meet his stepmother and stepsisters for the first time. His first impression is that they are too "Indian," meaning too uncultured in the modern ways of America. His father, unapologetic about marrying so soon after his wife died, explains that he could no longer stand to be alone in the big house.

At first everything his new family does irritates him. His father is no help smoothing the transition, doing little more than tell him to get along with his step-family. Then, after a trip to a Dunkin' Donuts alone with the two girls, he feels they aren't so bad. He sees their naiveté as a cute way of looking at America and its luxuries, for even a Dunkin' Donuts is luxurious to them.

As he softens his attitude toward his new family members, he's also increasingly angry at his father for abandoning all memories of his mother, even to the point of boxing up all photos of her. When one night he is babysitting the two girls, he finds the two going through the box of photos of his mother. Enraged, he grabs the box, screams at them, and roughly shoves one to the ground. He takes the box and leaves. He drives aimlessly for days, finally finds a suitable place where he buries the box of photos.

Months later he sees his father and new family again. Nothing is mentioned of his outburst and violence. The girls apparently never talked about it with their mother or his father. The girls have changed in those few months. They look at him without their wide-eyed naiveté. They don't seem to be afraid of him, but neither will he ever be part of their lives.

Kumiko says, "It's hard to believe that he could be so violent toward the little girls. I understand that he had a hard time dealing with his mother's death, but why take it out on little girls?"

"He's not a sympathetic character, is he?"

She wrinkles her nose. "Not at all. I don't like him."

"Why?"

"He's self-centered, immature. Old enough to understand what he's doing."

"Did he change for the better because of the incident?"

She thinks, sips from her beer. "I don't think so. He didn't even apologize the next time he sees them. He believes he did the right thing."

"I don't know about the 'right thing,' but he does seem to have justified what he did. Right or wrong."

"I suppose so. I just can't stop thinking about those poor girls. They changed because of the incident."

"Changed in a good way or bad way?"

"He forced them to stop being little girls. He forced them into no longer trusting anyone. It's kind of scary that we can so totally change someone else's life by a single brief action."

I nod. "I suppose we all have some incident that is such an event.

Something that is the dividing line between childhood and adulthood."

Kumiko says, "I agree. What is yours?"

I laugh. "You know me well enough. I'm still a kid. How about you?"

"It was when my boyfriend came to visit me here. I knew I'd changed a lot leaving L.A. when I left him. I knew I'd left the young me behind then."

*

IN THE MORNING, I wake up before Kumiko. She'd stayed up late, working on her translation. I finished a couple of beers and the horse mackerel before I fell asleep to the TV with its volume turned on low. I didn't wake up when she turned off the TV and lights and crawled into bed.

With my breath stinking of beer and fish, I'm still thinking of the short story. It's the kind of story that sticks in your head. Maybe because I see myself in the main character: self-centered and immature. At least I don't have a violent streak in me—I can't see me ever pushing a little girl around.

I think about Kumiko and her admission about the dividing line between childhood and adulthood. I try to imagine what it was like to clearly see that point, see one part of her life from the vantage point of another. Maybe that's what my grandfather saw when his adopted parents were swept away.

The story of his life in Japan also sticks in my head. I haven't done anything with it yet, other than the poor start to a poem. I should write it down, send it to my parents, aunts and uncles, cousins. But I haven't been able to do it yet. Maybe I never will.

I get dressed in the dark—the shades are blocking out the early light— and go down to the lobby. I ask the desk clerk directions to the nearest place for coffee and doughnuts. The story we'd read last night got me craving a doughnut. The front desk guy tells me of a couple of places. I ask if he wants me to bring him a doughnut or anything. He smiles, declines. I'm about to leave, when I think of something else to ask him. I pull out the photos of Yamazaki's tattoos.

"I'm trying to find a tattoo parlor that would do this kind of art."

He glances at it and says matter-of-factly, "That's local yakuza."

177

28.

Kumiko says, "yakuza, huh?"

"That's what he said. But just because Yamazaki has a yakuza tattoo doesn't mean he's yakuza, does it?"

"I don't know anything about yakuza."

"Me either. Except for what I've seen in movies. And I'm sure reality is far different."

"Of course. So what are we going to do?"

"If he is yakuza, then the police would have a record of him. An address, family members, his yakuza associates."

"I doubt the police will give us that kind of information."

"Good point. Any other ideas?"

"How about tattoo parlors? If we could find the place where he got the tattoo, they might have information about him."

"Brilliant," I say. "There can't be that many tattoo parlors, can there?"

"I don't know. But let's get started."

*

The desk clerk helps us make a list of the tattoo parlors in the area. The closest one to the hotel is in a rundown neighborhood of bars and massage parlors. The parlor isn't open yet. We find the second not too far away and it's just opening up. A blurry-eyed woman with pink hair and piercings and,

OH!

of course, tattoos, is sweeping the floor. She yawns and says "What about it?" when I ask her about the tattoo and show her the picture.

"A friend of mine had this tattoo. I'm trying to find where he got it."

"Why don't you ask him?" she says.

"We've lost touch over the years."

She squints at me then at the photo. "Not here. That looks like Blink-Blink."

Kumiko checks our list and shows it to me. Blink-Blink is on it. "Thanks," I tell the pink-haired parlor employee.

She shrugs and goes back to her sweeping.

Blink-Blink isn't open either so we get an early lunch at a noodle stand. Kumiko asks me to read the first few paragraphs of her translation. "It reads well to me," I tell her, honestly so. "But I'm no expert in the nuances of translations, or even in fiction."

"That's okay. As long as you think I've grasped the meaning of the English."

"You've done that."

We finish our noodles and walk around the neighborhood until the tattoo parlor opens and we go in. The walls are covered with photos of customers' tattoos, sample designs. The only employee is a man in his mid-thirties wearing a tiger-striped t-shirt with no sleeves. His arms are tattooed, his head shaved, and he sports a thin, long goatee. He gives us a questioning look — I guess we aren't his usual customers or maybe he doesn't get them this early in his workday.

Kumiko shows him the photos, saying she is looking for a long-lost cousin, our cover story concocted over noodles.

He glances and immediately says, "Yamazaki." Then he looks at Kumiko and says, "You haven't heard?"

"Heard?"

The tattoo artist scratches the back of his head. "Yamazaki, hmm, ... he committed suicide. A few months ago. I'm sorry."

Kumiko does a good job of acting surprised. "I didn't know," she says. "What happened?"

He says, "How much do you know about your cousin?"

"Not much. Really nothing since he was a little kid. I've just moved

180

here to Tokyo. All I had to go on are these photos of his tattoos he sent another cousin."

The tattoo artist frowns. "I don't know a lot about him. Just what we'd talk about during a session."

"That's okay," Kumiko says. "Anything. Be honest."

"Okay. Honest. He was trying to get into a local branch of the yakuza."

"So he wasn't actually a yakuza?" I ask.

"No. He was associated with some guys just one step up from juvenile delinquents." He gives Kumiko an apologetic glance. She gives him a reassuring nod to go on.

"They would do a few things to try to get the attention of the yakuza guys. Small crimes like stealing bikes, or errands like delivering packages or posting flyers for call girls. Most of the kids never amount to anything, as a criminal or otherwise. Yamazaki was more serious about his criminal career."

I say, "That's why he got the tattoos?"

"Whenever he had some spare cash, probably from selling shoplifted goods, he'd come back for another session. Maybe once a month. Maybe two or three times in a good month." He points to the photo. "You can see where we stopped.

"Yamazaki got his big break. What he thought was going to be his big break. He had caught the eye of one the lower minions of the local gang. This guy asked Yamazaki to get a job in a certain pachinko parlor. Which he did. His duties were cleaning up, emptying ashtrays, that kind of thing. Yamazaki even got a nickname: 'Pachinko Boy.'

"The gang was planning a big heist and were using Yamazaki for inside information about where the money goes, when they make transfers, which doors are locked, which are open. I'm not sure what they got Yamazaki to find out for them.

"So it's coming down to the big day and somehow the police get wind of the heist. I didn't hear how they found out about it, maybe an informant. Of course, the cops find out about the gang's inside man—Yamazaki.

"The cops haul him in. I heard that he didn't say a thing for two days. But eventually they break him down and he spills the story. I never saw Yamazaki again and the next time I heard about him was that he'd committed suicide in that car." He looks at Kumiko.

"Thank you for telling me," she says.

The tattoo artist says, "The bad thing … the crime gang would have gotten convicted anyway. Forcing a confession out of Yamazaki didn't really add much to their case. He didn't really need to kill himself. The whole thing was a bungled job from the beginning."

*

BACK IN THE HOTEL room in the evening, we're exhausted from traipsing around the neighborhood, not sure what to do after talking to the tattoo artist at Blink-Blink. He wouldn't give us the names of any of Yamazaki's old gang members. He said they wouldn't like strangers poking around asking questions. I didn't need too much persuasion to agree. The artist didn't know if Yamazaki had family in the area, or if he had a girlfriend. We thanked him and said if we were going to get tattoos we'd come to him. That made him happy.

I ask Kumiko, "Do you think Yamazaki killed himself over the botched robbery?"

She looks up from her translation practice. "He was obsessed with joining this gang and everything went wrong."

"I think so too."

"It's too bad," she says. "I got the feeling from the tattoo guy Yamazaki was a nice guy."

"A nice guy?"

"For a criminal anyway. Maybe nice is the wrong word. He was dedicated, did what the gang asked him to do. He didn't want to confess even when the police can make anyone confess."

"You're right. 'Nice' describes him well."

Narrow alleys and dark ~~streets~~ places.
Stairs going up, or is it down?
Into the corners of a mind,
~~into~~ finding the end of time.

29.

THE RAINY SEASON IS officially over, so now it's pouring rain. Apparently rainy season gives way to typhoon season. I'm sitting in my apartment, the TV on a cooking show. I haven't cooked for months. My weight dropped maybe ten pounds when I first got here. Now I've gained back that plus another five I'd guess. Maybe closer to ten. I haven't weighed myself. I'd go for a run, but not in this weather.

I'm reading Kumiko's full translation of the short story about the college student. Reading it in Japanese is a completely different experience from the English version. The language difference of course is there, but I can also see a Japanese sensibility about relationships. For one thing, having a step family in Japan is rare, even with divorce on the rise.

Seen through the lens of *mono no aware*, the main character has a sudden and intense realization of the tragedy behind his mother's death when he sees the girls going through the box of photos. He does not know how to deal with the painful sadness he feels at her death, and the seeming denial of her existence by his father. Instead of dealing with his feelings as a poet might, he lashes out at the girls.

It's all complicated by the character's craving for doughnuts.

While it's been raining for two days, I've been working on my artwork, a nice diversion. The pieces are kind of like watercolors, only with water applied to the art after the color is placed on the paper. Also, the technique works well in this rainy weather.

I've been working on my poetry. I bought a book on writing poetry, Western poetry, if you can call non-Japanese poetry "Western." Western poetry sounds like it would be written by cowboys. I'm not sure what the distinguishing characteristics would be in referring to Western vs. Eastern/Asian poetry.

Anyway, I believe I'm progressing, mainly because it's easier to write Western poetry. It's more like prose in a way, more directly stated. Still there are many of my attempts which land like rocks dropped onto mud—they plop with a thud and spray chocolate-water.

I do best when I concentrate on poetic acts, rather than poetry, with a capital P. In other words, focus on the expression, what sounds best, without a preconceived constraint of form.

I wonder if that's what the suicide victims were intending to accomplish—an expression of whatever they were feeling. Did they have something to say but couldn't find the words, or the art? Or did they simply want to end the pain?

The smiling TV chef lowers a lobster into a pot of boiling water.

*

DESPITE THE WEATHER, I'M meeting the professor at his favorite bar. On the way there, my umbrella didn't do much good and I'm soaked before I get very far. But it feels good to get out of the apartment. And I need to eat something sooner or later.

For the first time, the mama-san bar feels cozy. Before, its sparse furnishings, sharp lines, and other Japanese minimalist design made the bar feel on the cold, sterile side. Tonight for some reason, it's as if there's a fireplace and, in front of it, a dog curled on a rug.

The professor is talking with Mama-san when I enter and stick my umbrella in the holder at the front door. She gives out her welcoming shout while the professor waves and pulls out the empty stool next to him. I have a whiskey-water poured and placed in front of me before I can settle onto the stool.

"You got wet," Mama-san says and hands me a dry towel.

"I'm glad the rainy season is over," I say, and that makes them laugh.

The professor asks Mama-san to bring over a third glass of whiskey-water for her. She does and he raises his glass. I raise mine. She raises hers. He clinks his against mine and hers. "The paper is in the mail. Thank you for your help."

"Congratulations," I say.

"Congratulations," Mama-san says.

*

THE PROFESSOR AND I are the only ones left in the bar. Mama-san locked us in while she made an emergency run home to see to her ailing mother. We've gone over to a table so we can kick back and relax more than we can on the stools. We've gone through about half a bottle of whiskey. We've eaten several dishes of food, working our way through most of Mama-san's menu. We're sated, sipping our drinks. We don't care about the rain and wind, the flooding in low-lying areas, the erosion and mudslides.

After a long silence, I say, "I'd like to join your poetry club."

The professor makes no sudden move in surprise. He says nothing for several moments then looks at me with a hint of a smile. "I thought that might be you. One of our members said there was a young man lurking around the building. But how did you know it is a poetry club?"

"Sorry, I went inside and listened. Only for a few minutes."

"How did you know where I was going?"

"I happened to see you walk past the train station when you said you were going back to the university. I followed you."

He sips his drink. "I'm sorry to act suspicious. It's not that I'm trying to hide something from you. It's that our group is private."

I feel badly and wish I hadn't brought it up. "I don't mean to intrude."

He shakes his head. "I don't mean to imply that you wouldn't be welcome. Our group is ... I suppose I should tell you the truth. All of the members have suffered a tragedy, a loss, something we can't forget or get over. My tragedy is my daughter's disappearance when she was sixteen. Six years ago. She simply vanished one afternoon. There was no evidence that she was kidnapped. And because she'd run away once before, even though it was only for a day and over a minor tiff, the police believe she ran away.

"We searched for weeks. We talked to her friends, to her teachers. She played *go*, so we talked to her coach. No one had a clue. I don't think I slept for a week. I got horrifically ill and ended up in the hospital for several days. When I got out, my wife couldn't stand to see me. I reminded her that our daughter is gone. She blamed me for her running away. We eventually divorced."

He takes a sip of diluted whiskey. "The poetry club, for me, helps me understand what happened. Maybe it will help find her someday. Maybe it will help me … I don't know."

We sit in silence.

A person might feel sadness toward a thing,
but a thing cannot have an intrinsic, or
innate, sadness. A person has to interact in
a particularly meaningful way with the thing
for sadness to be experienced. For example,
why are a cricket's chirps characterized as
lonely? We don't for sure know why a cricket
chirps, nor do we know what it feels while it
chirps. Perhaps the cricket is happy, or hungry,
or lustful. For all we know, it could be feeling
nothing.

From the point of view of the poet, the sound of
the chirp resonates as a sad sound and most
people would likely agree. Similarly, certain
musical tones are perceived as sad or happy,
dark or light, in most listeners. The sound a
cricket makes is a tone we typically perceive as
lonely. If so, our perception and interpretation
of the tone makes it sad, rather than the chirp
being intrinsically sad.

30.

I'M IN THE PARISIAN Café, comparing the original short story and Kumiko's latest draft translation. I made a few suggestions on the first draft and talked with her about them. I told her I thought her translation was right on, but I'm no expert in literature—English, Japanese, or otherwise. I should give her translation to the professor to read. He has the ear for language, the intellect and insight for unraveling psychological narrative. He knows *mono no aware*.

Thinking about the professor reminds me that he didn't invite me to join his poetry club. Maybe because my poetry skills are too lame. Maybe because I've never experienced a tragedy as required for admittance. I wonder if my grandfather would count. Not so much his death, which at eighty-seven is not a tragedy, but his tragedy watching his parents drown. True, it's not my personal tragedy but at least it's in the family.

The professor wouldn't tell me exactly the specific tragedies the other club members had suffered, so I'm not sure what counts. But I'm curious. I'd like to hear what happened to the members, how they are dealing with it through poetry. Maybe the professor will offer an invitation some day.

I put away Kumiko's translation and the story, stop thinking about the professor's poetry club. Instead, I take a gulp of the lukewarm coffee and concentrate on the last of the four suicide victims: the only woman in the group, Junko Miyake, thirty-one, a Tokyo resident, occupation listed as "performance artist." We left the most difficult search for last. I hope Kumiko has come up with something else that will help us.

So far what we've learned about the three other victims is that they likely had very different reasons for joining the club. One guilty over the accidental death of a friend. One depressed over unrequited love. One shamed for failing his audition as a yakuza. Three reasons difficult to fully understand why they would cause a person to kill themselves.

Kumiko arrives more than an hour late. Clumped strands of hair drape across her face. "Sorry," she chimes as she brushes back the stray hair. "I've been on the phone."

"No problem," I say. "Everything okay?"

"Okay? Sure. Okay."

She doesn't elaborate and I don't press her. "May I get you a cup of coffee?"

She shakes her head. "I can't stay. I've got a few things to take care of."

"When will you be finished?"

"Probably not today."

"Oh."

She frowns. "I'm going to be busy for a while. Can you wait?"

I could but I don't have much else to do with my life. "Don't worry. I can get started and when you are free and want to help, just let me know."

She looks grateful.

*

I GO TO TOKYO by myself and check into the Crowne Plaza, Ikebukuro. It's not cheap but less expensive than most hotel rooms in Tokyo. The big room with a big bed and big TV connected to cable is worth it. After a soak in the tub with the TV blaring CNN, I order room service: a turkey sandwich with potato salad and a root beer float.

I'm feeling good, buoyant. Must be the root beer float. When I finish the meal, I go down to the lobby dressed in my Tokyo night outfit: clean jeans, white shirt, light jacket. In the lobby, I ask the concierge where to find some performance art.

He's youngish, blonde, with an Australian or New Zealand accent. "We don't get many requests for performance art. Do you mean something like *butoh*?"

"I've heard of it but have never been to a performance. It's a form of dance, right?"

"*Butoh* is a kind of unstructured dancing, transforming the artists into tortured forms. Thematically, the dance arises out of a post-WWII reaction to the horror of war. There isn't much of it around anymore, at least not in Japan. It's actually more popular in North America and Europe."

A wealth of information, isn't he? "I don't think so," I say. "I'm looking for something more contemporary."

"Let's see," the concierge looks at his computer screen. "There are a few small theaters putting on independent productions, but I don't think you'd call what they do 'performance art.' I'd probably be sending you on a wild goose chase."

"Let me ask you this, is there anything in your database there for a performance artist named Junko Miyake?"

It takes him two or three minutes to complete the search. "No, but my database is limited to established artists. You might try Yoyogi Park. Several groups and individual artists outside the mainstream perform there. It's not far from where the bands play on Sundays at Harajuku. I'm sure you've heard of that spectacle. Do you know how to get there?"

"Yes. Thanks," I say.

He shrugs. "Don't expect too much, mate."

*

It's SATURDAY NIGHT AND Harajuku is crowded with young people. Really young. I feel like an old man. I ended up in Harajuku one Sunday afternoon and watched the bands play and the dancers dance on a bridge across from the station. Most were good in an over-practiced, imitative way. A couple of them were very good in an original, unrehearsed way.

I take an easy stroll past the hip music places, chic boutiques, mobile phone stores. The people out this evening are either young or very young. More than half, I'd say, are dressed up as hip-hop artists, skater dudes, or cartoon characters. They seem to be in groups of three. Maybe two is not cool and four too unwieldy.

I find the edge of Yoyogi Park and a row of makeshift stages of tarps, cardboard boxes, beer crates, plywood. In one of the acts, three teenaged girls are dressed in the outfits of a popular girl band and are lip-synching to their music. A lone male dressed in a loin cloth and devil mask and a long red wig dances sensually to a boom box blurting out Japanese hip-hop. Another stage houses a small group dressed in black from head to toe. There are colored dots of luminescent paint on their fingers and other parts of their bodies. An ultraviolet light makes the dots glow when exposed. The group moves and the dots form patterns: a person walking a dog, a boy and girl kissing.

Another group of four is seated on four chairs arranged as if they are in a car. They are talking about life and their lives. They are dressed in business suits like the ubiquitous salarymen of Tokyo. Then they grow quiet. One of them lights a charcoal hibachi.

31.

THE FOUR PERFORMANCE ARTISTS slump in their chairs, not moving, for a full hour. I can't tell if they are breathing from where I stand and wonder if they are actually dead. The audience comes and goes. Most spend only a few seconds before moving on. Only one other audience member, a young woman, stays for the full hour. She doesn't take her eyes off the imagined suicide.

The group ends their performance when the charcoal goes cold. The audience doesn't clap as the group stirs slowly to life and begins to dismantle their stage. Clapping does seem inappropriate given the theme. But also, we aren't certain the performance is over.

I can tell out of the corner of my eye that the young woman is looking at me. I turn slowly. "You stayed for all of it," she says.

"You too," I say. "What did you think?"

She gazes at me for a few moments. "I think it was tremendous, very thought provoking. Of course, it had to be very thought provoking, didn't it? Your thoughts were all that were left while they pretended to be dead."

I hadn't thought of that, but she's right. "I agree. Almost meditative. Hypnotic."

She nods seriously.

I ask her, "Do you know the artists?"

"No. I just happened to be walking past. I was with a couple of friends, but they didn't want to stay. Do you know the artists?"

"No. I was just walking past too."

We stand in silence for a few moments watching them pick up their props. I break the silence with: "I'd like to discuss their performance with you. Would you like to get something to drink or eat and do that?"

She hesitates then says, "Okay."

"Great! If you don't mind waiting a minute or two. I'd like to ask the group members if they know someone."

I talk to the closest one. His longish hair is pulled back in a ponytail. I tell him I enjoyed the performance. He gives me a blank look like he'd never been complimented before. I ask him if he's ever heard of a performance artist named Junko Miyake.

"Junko Miyake? No. Never heard of her." He asks the others. They shake their heads.

*

THE YOUNG WOMAN'S NAME is Miki. She's eighteen, nearly nineteen, she added. Having graduated from high school, she isn't sure what she wants to do with her life. She might go to a business college in the near future but is in no rush. Her family owns a delivery business and they work seven days a week, eighteen hours a day. There is nothing at the business she wants to do. She told me all that in a few minutes in my hotel room.

I haven't made a move on her or anything. It just seemed like a waste of a big hotel room not to come back here for our conversation. She accepted my reasoning without apparent skepticism. Before we left for the hotel, she called her friends and told them where she was going and not to worry about her. She laughed when she hung up. "They think I'm lucky."

I laugh at that too.

Earlier I called room service and ordered two repeats of my lunch. The waiter who delivered it was the same one who delivered my first meal. He didn't laugh or crack a joke about my second and third turkey sandwich and root beer float.

Miki spears a cube of potato. "What are you doing in Japan?" she asks then pops the potato in her mouth.

I give her a simplified rundown of my trip. She listens intently, as focused as she had been watching the performance art. You don't meet too many people with that much patience. I tell her of my interest in the suicides at Aokigahara.

When I finish she says, "That's why you were asking the guys back there if they know … what is her name?"

"Junko Miyake."

She repeats the name. "She was one of the four who died in the car?"

"Yes."

"I can't imagine actually doing it, can you?"

"No," I answer.

"I tried to imagine what it would be like during the performance." She gets up from the chair at the table. Taking her root beer float with her, she lies on the bed. "It's more comfortable here."

I join her. "It is more comfortable."

"At the performance I was testing myself," she says. "I wanted to see if I could last as long as they could, not moving, barely breathing."

"You did well," I say.

She smiles, clanks her spoon on the side of the glass to get the last bite of ice cream. "I did, didn't I? How about you? Were you testing yourself?"

I'm testing myself now lying next to her. I stir the foam at the bottom of my glass, all that's left of my float. "I was curious how long they were going to last pretending to be dead. An hour was much longer than I thought. Maybe fifteen minutes, I thought. But your idea is much more interesting."

She puts her float glass on the side table and picks up the TV remote. "Okay if I put on some music videos?"

"Sure."

She finds the channel, turns on her side, and snuggles into the bed. We watch and listen to the videos for a while. It's getting late, the last trains are about to make their runs.

Ever the gentleman, I ask, "Do you need a taxi home?"

She asks quietly, "Can I stay here?"

"What about your parents?"

"They won't even know I'm gone." She gets up and takes off her clothes to her underwear. She gets under the covers.

I do the same. The sheets are cool, her body warm. I wonder about the

199

professor's daughter, if this is how she went missing. Staying in strange hotel rooms.

Her voice barely audible, she says, "The biggest problem with suicide …"

I wait for her to finish but she's asleep.

Natural and spontaneous reactions are expressive. In other words, we find it very difficult to keep from talking to others about what we feel deeply, no matter whether it's something unusual, terrifying, or amusing. Our nature is to express what we feel, as well as to seek out, or at least turn our attention to, those moments that make us feel. When we do this, we are doing so because we have to express our feelings, not because we have other motives.

The writer who works closely with detail— studying characters' most trivial gestures in the imagined scene to discover exactly where the scene must go next—is the writer most likely to persuade us. Almost without knowing they're doing it, writers become alert observers and not merely for the detail of the way the office manager who is about to have an affair with her boss holds her coffee mug, but the meaning of the way she holds the mug and what it says about her personality, about her heart. And to do this is to understand the *mono no aware* of the moment.

32.

I'M WALKING HOME FROM the Numazu train station as the evening is turning into night. I spent another day and night in Tokyo attending performance art exhibitions and asking performers if they know Junko Miyake. One performer asked Junko's stage name. He said he would be more likely to know her stage name than her real name. Apparently all performance artists have stage names. Of course I don't know her stage name.

I kept thinking back to the suicide performance. It seemed like the performers must have known or heard about Junko Miyake. A performance artist dying in a suicide-club car must have inspired their performance. I got the feeling they didn't want to talk to me about her. I got the feeling they didn't want to talk at all. As if they were still in character—that is, dead.

Miki hung out with me all day before she went home in the late afternoon. We went back to Harajuku, hit some music stores, watched the amateur bands. While we were hanging out, I asked her what she was going to say about suicide before she fell asleep. She said she didn't remember. Then as she was saying good-bye, she suddenly remembered. "Oh, yeah, the biggest problem with suicide is that it is boring."

Boring. Huh. I asked what she meant and she said, "It would be boring to kill yourself. It's all over. It would be much more interesting to stick around and see what happens."

I couldn't argue with that. I mean, I could have argued that suicide victims want to end their pain. From what I've seen so far, the suicide victim gets trapped in another world with an alternate logic. Death becomes the only answer to every question and situation. Death becomes the inescapable conclusion. Miki's logic is the opposite—suicide would be the worst thing that could happen.

My last sight of Miki was of her walking to the subway station, her pace languid, dismissive, as if she didn't want to go home but had nowhere else to go.

*

I'M WALKING PAST THE police box near the station, averting my eyes, walking quickly but not too quickly. As if I have an appointment, a legitimate purpose. I don't know that the police are looking for me still, but I don't want to make their job of picking up foreigners who've overstayed their visas any easier.

Safely past the police box, I slow down, not all that excited to be home. Not because of the surroundings, not because my apartment is the size of a suitcase, not because there's no room service with turkey sandwiches. It's because I might possibly end up staying here for years, maybe the rest of my life. What else is there? Where would I go and what would I do? Like a suicide victim, I'm trapped in my own weird logic.

What had I accomplished since I came here? Some things, sure. I found my grandfather's history here, discovered the tragedy that forced him to leave Japan and find a new life. I found the professor and *mono no aware*, that intriguing idea behind perception and emotion and expression. I met Kumiko. That's all good but I'm nowhere near satisfying the ultimate goal. Perhaps the longer I stay, the further I get from my goal.

I am trapped in my own logic. My own circular logic.

I stop at the liquor store vending machine, buy a can of cold beer, then climb up the stairs to my apartment. I hear footsteps on the stairs behind me, but that's not unusual. Likely it's a couple of customers on the way to the karaoke bar or the yakitori restaurant. When I get to my door, get out my key, I hear the footsteps still following me. Maybe I will actually meet some of my neighbors.

With a smile on my face, I turn to see two police officers filling the space on the landing.

204

*

I'M IN A ROOM with stark walls, a table, chairs, no window. My bag and beer—the latter no longer cold—sit on the table. I think about drinking the beer despite its temperature. A police officer stands behind me. I've been in the police station for about twenty minutes so far. The officers haven't told me what I'm being hauled in for. One of them rifled through my bag, finding only dirty clothes, a toothbrush, and a couple of books.

Finally, a detective or inspector or whatever they call them here comes in. He has my passport, which he sets in front of him as he sits across from me. "You speak Japanese, huh?"

"Yes, a little."

"A little, huh?"

"Yes."

"Okay, Hara. Zack Hara. We brought you here because, one, you have overstayed your tourist visa. Two, you stole a bottle of whiskey from the One-Two Bar in your apartment building. Three, you worked illegally at Zenon English Academy. Do you confess?"

He gets right to the point, doesn't he? "Don't I get an attorney?" I say.

The detective shakes his head. "This is Japan. We can hold you ten days without an attorney."

Yikes. "But how do I know my rights?"

He grins. "You should have thought of that before you committed the offenses. So confess!" He slams his hand on the table and I jump a few inches out of my chair.

I don't know how he could know that I pilfered a bottle from the karaoke bar's storage closet. I drank the evidence, got rid of the bottle. Except for the label. Oh shit. But how could they know where the label came from? I'm not even sure I have it any more. Maybe someone saw me. And as for teaching illegally, well, I don't want to get the director, shacho, in trouble. There is no evidence that I worked there, unless my students told them.

"We have evidence," he says in a calm almost bored voice, as if he read my mind.

I say, "Yes, I overstayed my visa. I will confess to that. Obviously you have the evidence right here." I point to my passport. "The overstay is an oversight on my part. I would like to get an extension if possible. However, I can't confess to numbers two and three."

"We have evidence."

"What evidence?"

"The usual. Fingerprints, witnesses, video."

All that for a couple of petty offenses? I doubt it.

He says, "Come on, confess."

"Look," I say. "I'm sorry, I overstayed my visa. I'll be happy to get the situation fixed. But I really don't know where you got your information about the other offenses. I'm not guilty."

The detective eyes me for several seconds. I force myself to return his gaze, calmly, not forcefully. He gets up and leaves.

The can of beer is looking better all the time. I wish I knew the penalties for theft or illegal employment. Overstaying a tourist visa by a couple of months seems a minor infraction.

After ten minutes the detective returns. We repeat the interrogation almost word for word. I repeat my story almost word for word. He leaves again. Then he comes back in after fifteen minutes. He belches. It smells like ramen. We go through the interrogation again with the same results. It's like water-drip torture. No wonder Japanese police solve ninety percent of their cases through confession. He leaves and comes back in twenty minutes.

This time he says, "We are going to let you go pending further investigation. You can't leave Numazu until the matter is resolved. You will need to submit a visa extension within forty-eight hours or face a deportation hearing. But you need to have a sponsor to vouch for you while you do that. Is there someone who can be your sponsor?"

I give him the professor's name.

Questions with no answers.
Truth—the absence of lies.
I fold my umbrella,
hoping the rain has ended.

33.

I'M AT THE AMERICAN Bar and Grill nursing my first beer. Nursing it because I'm trying to make my funds last. I have enough to last a month or so. Unless I need an attorney. I'm not yet clear on all the legal implications of my run-in with the police. I was shaken by the ordeal although I can't see myself incarcerated for my petty crimes. I could see myself paying restitution to the bar (what, fifty dollars?) then getting deported. That's not the worst thing in the world, although I'm not ready to leave Japan.

Anyway, I'm free for the moment. The professor offered to be my temporary sponsor until I get my visa extended. He didn't seem too concerned about my criminality. Not to mention he was partially responsible for one of the crimes, at least for putting the idea in my head. I doubt if I would have pilfered from the bar in the first place if he hadn't assigned the task of committing a petty crime.

At one point in my ordeal, the thought crossed my mind that I was in serious trouble because of Miki. I don't know the legal age of consent in Japan, but I think eighteen would be it. Unfortunately, I only had her word she is eighteen, "nearly nineteen." To be honest, it's hard for me to tell young women's ages, here or elsewhere. She could have been fourteen for all I know.

On the other hand, we didn't actually do anything except sleep together. I mean nothing sexual happened. She just wanted to sleep. I suppose having her stay in my hotel room could be construed as kidnapping in some overzealous prosecutor's eyes. All she had to do was complain I held her against her will, enticed her up to my room with the offer of a root beer float. They would produce a grainy, black-and-white, date-stamped closed-circuit tape showing me and Miki entering the lobby, catching the elevator, entering my room. Another tape would show us leaving the next morning. What happened during the ten hours or so between the two tapes would be obvious to anyone.

Geez, I'm acting paranoid.

*

Kumiko comes into the bar and sits next to me. "Are you okay? I heard you were arrested."

"There's nothing to worry about. I overstayed my visa. I'm trying to get it extended."

"I heard there were other charges. Shoplifting or something?"

"Oh that. Not shoplifting no. But it's something I can take care of."

She gazes at me, judging my veracity. "Everything is okay then? I'm glad to hear it."

"Me too. I'll get you something to drink if you want."

"I'll have a Chu-Hai."

"Anything to eat?"

"Maybe we could split a seafood salad if you want?"

"Sure."

*

When I return with her drink, she's talking on her phone. She ends the call. "So how was Tokyo? Did you find the performance artist?"

"Without you along, I didn't have any good luck."

She laughs. "I'm not lucky. Not good luck anyway. But this might help." She reaches into her bag and takes out a photograph. "Meet Junko Miyake. My reporter friend got it from one of his detective buddies in the police department."

The photo is a head shot, a slightly blurred copy of a photo ID. It's not

210

the best but better than nothing. She has a thin, serious face. Her eyes are large and that's what I'd describe as her distinguishing feature.

"Thanks! When I get my visa extended, I'll go back to Tokyo with the photo. I found some performance artists when I was there who might recognize her picture. Would you like to go with me? Bring me some luck?"

She frowns, looks down. "I better tell you this now. I'm not too excited about this stuff with the suicide victims anymore. It's like kind of depressing. No, it's very depressing."

I hadn't considered that. I should have. "I'm sorry."

"It's not your fault. I thought searching for the suicide victim's stories would be interesting and something fun to do with you. Especially after what I went through in Tokyo. And it was fun and interesting. I had a good time with you, especially talking about fiction and working together on that short story. But ... well, I started thinking about the suicide victims too much. They are getting into my head. I don't know ... it's all just too much."

"Sure, I understand completely. I'll never bring it up again."

She smiles weakly, takes a sip of her drink. "I did do one other thing while you were in Tokyo. Consider it my going away present from the project." She takes out a sheet of paper from her bag. "You remember the website where the four met? I had the tech guy at my office job look up the ownership in the domain name registry. This is the website's owner's name, address, phone number in Tokyo. Maybe he knows something more about Junko Miyake." She gives me the paper.

I skim through it. "Thanks. This should help."

"Speaking of Tokyo," Kumiko says. "I've got some other news. The company I work for is expanding in Tokyo and offered me a job there. I think I'm going to take it. The job isn't in literary publishing, but if I'm in Tokyo at least I'm one step closer."

"That makes sense. When will you leave?"

"In a couple of days."

"Wow. That is soon."

*

WE END UP BACK in my apartment, sitting on my ratty futon. I want to say that I'll miss her. But it doesn't sound like the right thing to say for some reason. And it reminds me of my fumbling farewell to Carine. Look at how that ended up—she and Joe together. No telling what will happen if I tell Kumiko I'll miss her. Besides, I don't think she will miss me. So why put pressure on her to lie?

I'm not very good at this goodbye stuff, am I?

Of course, it's a good thing she's getting away. I've become morose, a downer. I realize if I was the least bit sensitive, I would have sensed our research on suicide victims was depressing her. To me, it's just one more task assigned to me by the professor.

Watching her gaze at the wall, I think she knows this is our last time together. I wonder if she told herself not to fall in love with me like she did with her L.A. boyfriend. I doubt she needed to. I never felt she loved me. As for me, I do feel something for her. Different from how I feel about Carine. But I'm not sure what it is. More … I really don't know.

Geez, I need to lighten up. Forget all this crazy stuff about *mono no aware* and suicide clubs and art and poetry. I need to become Joe. His only worries are coffee beans and chic cigarettes and writing a screenplay.

I'm not sure what we should be doing—saying farewells, reminiscing, drinking, screwing. But we just sit on my ratty futon.

34.

MY VISA WAS EXTENDED for another thirty days. The professor, my sponsor, went with me to the visa office. The severe-looking bureaucrat wasn't too happy about giving me the extension, but the professor was able to convince him that I posed no threat and have a legitimate cultural reason for staying longer. The professor gave the bureaucrat a mini-lecture on what I was doing to absorb culture and philosophy. He mentioned the poem I wrote upon discovering the story of my grandfather. He talked about *mono no aware* and how I was reading about Motoori Norinaga. Finally, the agent groaned and waved his hands in surrender. With a vicious thump, he stamped my passport, scrawled in the dates of the extension, and tossed it back to me.

Now I'm at the professor's office. He's called me in to do another round of tests. It's the least I can do for him. I'm wired up and I'm reading some poetry. I recognize a few of them from the first test. The rest of the poems are new to me but along the same genre as the others, Japanese poetry dealing with *mono no aware*.

After the poems the professor tells me to relax and imagine a series of situations that he will give me one at a time. The first situation he gives me is getting lost in the Aokigahara Forest. Thinking about it, my first feeling is that it seems to have happened so long ago. I try to imagine the moment I felt lost, how I found my way out, meeting the farmer with the shovel.

The next is finding the pear-shaped stone; I linger on the moment when I realize the shape of an Asian pear would satisfy the task as much as a harder to find Western pear. The next is the petty crime. I'm sure that will get a big response from his machines—I'm thinking of the arrest more than the crime itself.

The next images I'm to conjure up are the four suicide victims: the attorney Murano, the factory worker Kudo, the gang wannabe Yamazaki, the performance artist Miyake. One at a time I think of them sitting in the car at Aokigahara. One at a time I imagine where they sit, front or back seat, driver or passenger side. I imagine what they might have been feeling, thinking, as they drew their last few breaths. I see the tree clinging to the rock cliff, their last sight. My thoughts stray to Miki, standing beside her for an hour watching the performance suicide, our night at the hotel eating turkey sandwiches and drinking root beer floats, our day spent just walking around Tokyo. I think of Kumiko, how I let her down by not knowing how our search was affecting her. I think about how I haven't been a very good friend or lover or whatever we are. Then I think of Carine and how I let her down as well, how she met Joe at my going away party ...

"Finished," the professor says. He turns off the machines and starts to unplug me.

I ask him what the measurements show.

"I will let you see them eventually. But for now, I don't want you to think about the measurements, only to think about your relation to objects and events in the world."

"All of them?"

"No, I mean pick meaningful ones. Think about them. Feel them. Do your art. Work on your poetry."

*

"ARE YOU STILL LOOKING for your daughter?" I ask the professor.

He doesn't answer right away. We are sitting in his office, drinking tea and eating thin rice crackers with a soy sauce glaze sprinkled with flecks of roasted seaweed.

"I think about looking for her but I don't know where to start. I don't know if I have the energy. I looked a lot at first, of course. It consumed my life."

"What would happen if you found her?"

Again he thinks for a long time. I snap a piece of cracker in my mouth, breaking the silence.

"That's a good question. I don't know. It's been so long and so much has happened." He takes a drink of tea. "Of course, I want to know if she is okay. Healthy. Living comfortably."

"You don't want her to be suffering."

"Of course."

"Do you want to know why she ran away?"

He opens his mouth to say something, changes his mind, and says, "That's not important. It's all in the past."

"But if it affects the present?"

He doesn't answer. His boyish face grows old and serious as we talk about his daughter.

I ask, "Does the poetry club help?"

He brightens a little. "I can say that it does."

"Why do you meet in secret?"

"It's not that much of a secret. But yes, I would agree it's, um, ... secretive?"

The Word of the Day. "Yes. Secretive."

"We feel what we do is very private. That way we can be honest. Is dealing with grief much different in America?"

"I think it is. We like to show people grieving on TV. We like to see them cry and wallow. It makes great ratings because people want to see it. Maybe because they want to see raw emotion in people."

The professor nods. "I suppose it's the same here. We want to see emotion, real emotion, because we need a vicarious emotional experience without going through all the pain or even ecstasy ourselves."

"Vicarious emotions. Maybe so."

"The poetry club is different from that. We try to develop a deep, complex expression of our emotions. We provide a space mentally and physically to do it. We provide our own therapy in a country that looks down on therapy. We are able to explore the tangled threads of our feelings and find some sense and meaning."

I think about that for a while. "I hope to get to that point someday."

The professor sips his drink and says nothing.

Mono no aware applies to our understanding of human relationships. When someone sees another person deeply grieving, the observer empathizes in the grief. The observer is aware of the heart of the event, the affecting significance of the context. Being aware of the heart of the event that caused the person to grieve, the observer feels sympathy for that grief and is emotionally moved. On the other hand, someone who is not sensitive to *mono no aware* and so not aware of the heart of the sad event, has no sympathy for the other's grief, however acutely perceived. Norinaga makes a distinction between the emotions. Joy, he claims, is easily forgotten while grief and especially the pain of love is long-lasting.

35.

WITHOUT KUMIKO TO DISTRACT me, without editing work for the professor, the days get long. I think a lot. I drink a lot. I think about drinking a lot. I drink because I think a lot. When not drinking or thinking, I spend time in the coffee shop reading, working on poetry, sketching. My constantly gurgling stomach rebels at the quantities of coffee I pour down my throat.

Rationally, I should leave Numazu. The police haven't gotten around to arresting me yet and I should take off before they do. I'd be better off traveling, seeing new sights, meeting new people. Forget the crazy tests the professor is running. Forget writing poetry. Forget creating *mono no aware* art. Forget about suicide victims. Forget about Kumiko and Carine. Forget about the burgeoning tribe of cockroaches in my rabbit hutch apartment.

Create a blank slate. That's what I should do.

But I can't. I'm stuck here. I want to finish it out, finish wherever it's going to be. I want to complete my tasks, find out more about the suicide victims. I want to write a decent poem so full of *mono no aware* that the professor will be amazed. Maybe so much he'll let me in his secret, underground poetry club.

I don't know if I'm getting better at the poetry, but working on it is better than watching daytime drama or cooking shows. Better than sleeping until noon. My art is still better than my poetry. I'll keep at my poetry, work harder.

I heard from Carine via email. We hadn't corresponded since her visit. She says she is sorry it's been so long. Work has been crazy. Her promotion means more responsibilities for only a little more money. She mentioned the truck is okay. She didn't say too much about Japan, nothing other than she and Joe had a great time. She ended the email saying it was great to see me.

I guess that's all I need to know. I wrote her back with a short breezy email saying nothing about my legal troubles. Nor any of my other troubles. Of course, I tell her it was great to see her, and Joe of course.

Yesterday, I heard from Kumiko in a brief email. She found an apartment, sharing one with a couple of her co-workers. She's busy at the new job, sixteen hour days, only Sundays off, and then they often do required company-sponsored social outings. In other words, her life is completely full.

After reading that email, I feel the need to get out of town for a couple of days. Maybe to Tokyo, continue my search for information on Junko. She's been elusive so far. I did follow up with the suicide website information Kumiko found for me. I called the phone number but it was no longer in service, and the website no longer up. Another dead end in my search for Junko.

I'm tired of sitting so I pay my bill. The cashier is always glad to see me leave, can't imagine why. Outside, I walk to the ocean. It's a quiet afternoon, listless and breathless. Even a couple of dogs I pass on a little patch of grass in front of a home don't bother to bark at me.

I walk along the seawall. The light waves wash over the pebbles and stones, creating a mumbled sound like a hand swirling around in a sack of marbles. There are a couple of fishing boats in the distance. They aren't moving, not even bobbing up and down. It's like an oil painting.

I'm not really thinking of anything then I suddenly remember what I overheard the professor say at the meeting of his poetry club. Something about the ultimate *mono no aware* experience being at the moment before death. I suppose it would be, especially if it's true that your life flashes before your eyes. All of the events, all of the people, all of it compressed to a few seconds.

*

222

MAMA-SAN SERVES ME A beer and a dish of pickled veggies. The briny tidbits are better than pretzels or salty nuts when drinking beer. The professor isn't here tonight so I can drink beer.

"How are you?" she asks me.

"The same," I answer.

She gives a hearty, lusty laugh. "You always say that."

"I know. I'm sorry. Let's see … I'm not the same. I'm a little confused about something. It's about the professor. He seems depressed. But I don't know him that well, so it may be his normal demeanor."

She says, "No. The professor isn't depressed. He just thinks a lot. He's a great thinker. Maybe he's thinking more than usual."

I take a bite of pickle, let her know it's delicious with a smack of my tongue off the roof of my mouth. After a sip of beer, I say, "I wonder if he's thinking about his daughter."

"Why do you think that?"

"He told me the story about his daughter."

"It's sad, isn't it?"

"Very sad. Did he tell you why she might have run away? Was she having trouble at home, school?"

She hesitates, probably unsure what she should tell me. "I don't remember him mentioning trouble with her at home or in school. But he doesn't tell me everything."

"Did he mention that she ran away once before she disappeared?"

"I can't remember …" She looks away as if her memory was etched on the wall. "Once, I think. Yes, yes. Now I remember. She went all the way to Tokyo by herself. I think it was a year, maybe two, before she went missing. She wanted to go to Tokyo but got lost and eventually went to a station agent who called her parents."

"So the police believed she ran away again. This time successfully."

"Yes. There wasn't any evidence she was kidnapped."

"The professor must have been devastated."

"He was desperate to find her. I didn't see him for a few months, before he came back here. I remember it snowed that day. When I told him how sorry I was to hear about his daughter, he said, 'It's all over now. She's gone.'"

In Japan, the flowering cherry blossoms
represent the universal laws of nature, the
unending cycle of life: birth, death, rebirth.
Snow serves as a symbol of the world of winter,
darkness, and death, a foreshadowing of life to
come.

36.

WHILE MAMA-SAN TENDS TO her other customers, I think about my parents. On the whole, they are fine parents, neither too distant nor too intimate. When I was growing up, they never pushed me unreasonably regarding grades or activities or other life choices. They let me try things like Little League baseball, piano lessons, art lessons, Boy Scouts. And if I didn't like the activities or got tired of them and quit (which I eventually did with all of them), they never said anything. They didn't have to discipline me too many times. Even when I screwed up they were reasonable about punishments and lectures. I was a pretty good kid so maybe they had it easy as parents as much as vice versa. They didn't put on a real love fest — no hugs, not even a spontaneous "I love you," but I could sense some affection and respect.

The only reason I'm thinking about them now is that it's hard for me to imagine a kid running away from home at sixteen. The world is actually a pretty rough place at any age, let alone when you are so young. Something drastic must have happened in the Imai household.

Mama-san comes back to me, freshens my beer. I ask her if she ever met the professor's daughter.

"No, never," she answers. "I saw a photo of her. In fact ..." she disappears behind the counter for a moment, then pops back up and places a photograph on the counter. "I forgot I had this until just now. The professor left it here years ago."

It's a photograph of a teenage girl in a sailor-suit school uniform. She has long hair, her head tilted to one side in that cute pose Japanese school girls put on. I can see the professor's genes in her round face.

"She's beautiful," I say. "By the way, what's her name? The professor never told me."

"Noriyo."

"Noriyo," I repeat. I suddenly realize she looks a lot like Miki. Good-looking, in a soft, intelligent way. I remember Miki walking away from me toward the subway station in her easy, confident, almost aloof way. Maybe Noriyo turned her back on her parents in that same aloof way. "Did the professor ever say why he thought she went missing?"

Mama-san says, "We never discussed it."

I get the feeling she's not telling me the truth. Why would he give her a picture of Noriyo and then not talk about why she ran away? Maybe he was embarrassed. Another question comes to mind. "Has he always been a poet?"

"I know he writes poetry. He occasionally shows me a poem. I write a little myself, but I'm not good. He's very good. I think he started writing poetry after his daughter went missing. At least we didn't talk about poetry until then. Before then, he was a single-minded scientist. He had no hobbies other than coming here. Why?"

"Just curious. Not many scientists write poetry. I was wondering if his daughter's disappearance had anything to do with his poetry."

She laughs, a little nervous laugh, and leaves to help another customer.

*

IN THE MORNING, I arrange to meet the professor at his office. I tell him I have some questions about *mono no aware*. He has several meetings already but says he can spare a few minutes in the afternoon.

I've made a decision to assign myself a new task—find the professor's daughter. I don't want to come right out and tell him my plan. Obviously, he didn't want me to know about his daughter's disappearance. If I hadn't found out about his poetry club I might never have known about the tragedy which spurred him to write poetry. I need to approach the whole matter with some delicacy.

When he's free, the professor and I go outside in the fine early autumn afternoon. We walk along a path in a garden along the edge of the campus. He points out the highlights: a pond, a bonsai pine grove, an ancient wooden bridge.

I tell him I've been reading Motoori Norinaga's *The Sedge Hat Diary*. "It's got me thinking more about your daughter, strangely enough."

He thinks for a couple of steps, then shrugs. "Maybe not so strange. She's on a journey as well."

"Exactly. There are new sights to be seen, new people to meet. But the traveler can't help see the sights and people in the light of home, comparing them to what one has already seen and is familiar with."

The professor agrees. "Our brains seek recognizable patterns matching our previous knowledge with the current situation."

We walk a little further into the garden. "I'm trying to understand how Noriyo felt when she left her home, as well as what you felt when you realized she was gone. Strictly in the light of helping me understand *mono no aware*. I don't want to bring up any painful issues."

The professor waves his hand dismissively. "No. It's a good idea, I think."

"Thank you. When you have some time, maybe we could talk about it in depth?"

"All right. We could meet tomorrow tonight."

"That's fine. In the meantime, I would like to talk to a few other people. You mentioned a *go* coach? How about some of her friends or teachers?"

After another couple of steps, he says, "All right, I suppose that wouldn't be too intrusive. I can write some names for you when we get back in my office." He pauses, then says, "Good luck."

EXHIBIT W092

Norinaga's journey chronicled in *The Sedge Hat Diary* was not always a pleasant stroll through the cherry blossoms and mountains. At times the weather and poor roads created not only misery but fear. Once the wind blew so fiercely their sedge hats were ripped off their heads and the travelers feared losing their footing and tumbling into a gorge, down to their deaths.

37.

ONE OF NORIYO IMAI'S middle school teachers agreed to meet after school. I'm in his classroom, sitting at a student's desk while he sits behind his teacher's desk. Fumio Wada is about fifty-five years or so from retirement. Dark, puffy skin sags under his eyes. His skin is ashen. I think the next five years will kill him.

"Noriyo was one of those students who didn't stand out much," he says. "She didn't volunteer answers or to do something. But when asked she would answer or do whatever I asked. She never got into trouble. She was smart in a common-sense kind of way. If she didn't immediately know an answer, she could reason her way toward it."

"Did she have many friends?"

"She was neither very popular nor fodder for bullies."

"All in all, she sounds rather forgettable," I say. "Why do you even remember her at all?"

The teacher considers my question while he fiddles with the knot of his tie. "I suppose it's because I heard she went missing only three years after she was in my class. That event must have cemented her in my memory."

"What did you think about her disappearance?"

"I was surprised. She seemed the least likely person to go missing. I've had my share of students run away but there was always an obvious reason."

"Did you know her father?"

"I never met Professor Imai personally. Noriyo's mother came to student teacher conferences. But I remember nothing about her other than the fact that she came to the conferences."

"Do you recall Noriyo's interests? Anything that she might still be pursuing?"

He rubs his forehead. "Nothing I can recall. She was competent but not enthusiastic about any one thing, at least not in my class."

"I heard she played *go.*"

"I don't remember. But ask the coach. In fact, the *go* club is meeting now."

"Is this the same coach when Noriyo was here? Tetsuo Iwaki?"

He nods and rubs his forehead. I don't ask if I'm giving him a headache or if it's a chronic condition.

*

SIX GO BOARDS ARE set up in a classroom. At each, a pair of students are gazing intently at their board and current position. Every few seconds, one of the players picks up a black or white stone and places it on the board, making a sharp clicking sound.

The coach, Tetsuo Iwaki, stands next to one of the boards, his arms folded across his chest, watching a game. His hair is long, pulled back and secured into a ponytail. He wears a sweater over an unbuttoned collared shirt, casual slacks, and sneakers.

He sees me, says something to the pair he's watching, then walks over to me. When I introduce myself and tell him why I'm here, he raises an eyebrow and motions for me to follow him into an empty classroom.

"Noriyo Imai," he says with a soft voice. "I haven't heard about her lately. Has she been found?"

"Not that I know." I give him my little story about the professor being a friend, doing him a favor.

"What do you want from me?" he asks with a bite of impatience.

"Just some basic information about Noriyo, for instance, how long was she in the *go* club?"

"All three years she was here in this school."

"She liked the game a lot?"

"I think she enjoyed playing the game, particularly the last year when she could hold her own against the best players. She still lost more than she won but she was moving up in the rankings."

"So she wasn't a good player?"

"Noriyo wasn't the best, wasn't the worst, but she loved the game. I'd say she wasn't too bad her last year here. She moved beyond basic strategies to become a more creative player. Before then she was too predictable. Do you play *go?*"

"I've never played."

"Then I don't think you would understand the subtleties of expertise levels in the game." He gazes at me.

Nice guy. I change the subject. "Did you keep in touch after she went to high school?"

"No," he answers then adds, "I encourage my players to move on."

"Did she play in a high school club?"

"I have no idea."

"Would you have any idea of why she ran away? Assuming that's why she went missing."

"No, I wouldn't."

"According to her teacher, she was rather undistinguished in her studies. I wonder if you would characterize her using that term as well?"

"No. I wouldn't. If I had to come up with one term ... well, I'd say underdeveloped. But with great potential."

"Anything else about her that might be of help?"

"No."

I gaze at him for a long moment. "I'm wondering why the professor would give me your name."

"I have no idea." He steps toward the door and holds it open for us. "I need to get back to the club."

*

FINDING ANOTHER NAME ON the list, one of Noriyo's friends named Mariko Okayama, proves impossible. There are only two entries for Okayama in the phonebook. When I call, neither know of Mariko Okayama.

So far I haven't got much, if anything, to help me find Noriyo. The only thing the least bit suspicious was the *go* coach's attitude toward answering questions about her. He seemed to know more than he was telling me. But I wasn't sure what I expected to find out. Maybe some deep secret which would lead me to her. She seems to have been a regular kind of teenager.

Exhausted, I climb the stairs to my apartment. It's been a long day of running around. When I get to the top landing I see a stack of boxes. I open one and see some of my books and my travel bag.

38.

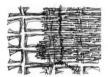

ACCORDING TO A NOTE from my landlord taped to my apartment door, I've been evicted. No reason is given but I'd guess it has something to do with my legal problems. I sit on the boxes, wondering what to do. First, I call the professor on my mobile phone and tell him I can't make our scheduled meeting. "I have to find a new place to stay. I've been evicted."

He tells me to wait while he drives over. I'm not sure what he has in mind. I bring the boxes down to the street where I sit on them and wait. I start to wish I hadn't called the professor. I should deal with my problems on my own. I should just pack up my bag and say good-bye to Numazu. Then I realize I didn't get to say good-bye to the clan of roaches. I hope they survive the new tenant.

The professor arrives in a few minutes. He drives a Toyota sedan big enough to haul my boxes. After we finish loading the car and drive away, he says I can stay with him until I find a new place.

"I really appreciate it," I say.

"No problem," he says. "Do you know why you were evicted?" he asks.

"My landlord is the brother-in-law of my old boss at the language school. I'm sure he found out about my trouble with the police."

"Probably," he says. "You can stay at my house as long as you need."

*

THE PROFESSOR'S HOME IS at the edge of town on the slope of a hill facing Suruga Bay. It's an older home with a silver-gray patina to the cedar siding. He tells me there's a view of Mt. Fuji when it's not cloudy.

Inside, the house smells of pine and straw mats. He shows me to a guest bedroom at the back of the house. A window looks onto a small Japanese garden. When the boxes are piled neatly in the guest room, he shows me the bathroom with a cypress soaking tub. He shows me the kitchen and tells me to help myself to the food. Then he takes me to a room with tatami mats and a low table and cushions. He tells me to relax while he fixes us a drink.

In a minute he returns with a flask of sake and two cups. A perfect drink in the old house.

"Your home is wonderful," I say.

"It's been in my family for over a hundred years," he says. "Drafty in the winter, hot in the summer, but it suits me. My wife hated it."

I see some photographs in frames on a shelf in a book case along the far wall. Pictures of Noriyo. I don't see one of his wife. "Why did she hate it?"

"She likes modern conveniences. Central heat and air. While we were married she told me weekly that the house is too hard to keep clean, too far from town, too far from Tokyo."

"But she left because of Noriyo? Isn't that what you said?"

"I think she could have put up with the house if Noriyo hadn't run away. She moved to Tokyo a year after Noriyo disappeared. She bought a brand new condo. I'm sure she's happy there."

"You keep in touch?"

"Only through a New Year's card. Always with the same, short message: 'No news.' I'm not sure what news she means."

"Did the police ever find anything about your daughter?"

"Nothing. They went through the motions of an investigation, nothing more than minimal effort. They told me over one hundred thousand teenagers run away or otherwise disappear each year. As if that statistic was supposed to be of comfort."

"I talked to one of her teachers and to her coach."

"I'm surprised they would talk with you. They didn't have anything to offer at the time and it's been so long."

"They said your daughter was a good student, a good *go* player. She was never any trouble. Neither could see that she was the type to disappear on her own."

"No one does," he says quietly. "No one."

*

I'M HAVING TROUBLE FALLING asleep. The house is too quiet, the room too comfortable, too big. I can stretch out and not hit a wall. There's no skitter of little roach feet. I reach over to a small floor lamp and turn it on. I read for a while until I throw on some clothes and quietly go into the kitchen. I poke around the cupboards and find a stash of instant noodles. While I heat up some water in an electric kettle, I read some more of *The Sedge Hat Diary*. During his journey, Norinaga stayed at inns, shrines, and homes of locals willing to put him up for the night.

The sights, events, and people Norinaga meets along the way remind him of poems he's read or inspires him to write his own. He doesn't say how long it takes him to write one, but he seems to dash them off effortlessly.

The water is ready and I fix the noodles, wait for them to cool.

In a way, I'm on a journey too, staying at inns, cheap rooms, and people's houses. I'm writing poetry too. The big difference between Norinaga's journey and mine is that I don't know what I will find when I get to my destination. Norinaga knew he'd find the cherry blossoms at his. I don't think there will be cherry blossoms at mine.

I dig into the noodles with a pair of the professor's chopsticks.

The word *aware* is believed to be derived from *appare*, an utterance similar to "Oh!" or "Ahh." *Aware* then became a noun that referred to those moments when one was so moved. The "ahness" of these situations was initially not limited to sadness, but used to express any emotion. Because sadness is deeply felt, *aware* became associated most closely with that emotion. Today, the word *aware* is most often associated with "pitiful" or even "wretched." For example: *awarena hito* means pitiable or wretched person.

39.

WHEN I FINALLY FALL asleep, I'm out until mid-morning. There isn't a rice packing plant firing up at dawn. No trains are running nearby. There's no traffic. The only noise comes from a couple of ravens squawking. The professor must have already left for the university. It feels delicious in my room in the old house, as if I were meant to live here in the solitude.

I stay on the futon for awhile then I get up and check the house. The professor is gone. He didn't leave a note but did leave a pot of coffee on the warmer. I help myself to a mug and take it into the garden. The morning is pleasantly warm, the sunlight filtered through a haze of humidity. Dew spots the leaves of the plants and blades of grass. The effect of the hazy sunlight and moisture softens everything, gives it an unfocused appearance.

In a sudden thought, I realize that is what's wrong with my poetry. I give everything a hard edge, a stark detail. My word choice is too literal. I need to look at things as if softened in haze, unfocused through a haze of emotion, through metaphor. I go back inside, ready to try some poetry along those lines.

In the hallway, I come to a room with the door shut. I can't resist the urge to look so I open the door and step in. The bed is covered with a plain rose-colored comforter. Along one wall is a bookcase. On its shelves are photos of Noriyo at various ages posed with and without her parents, a few textbooks, and two *go* strategy books. In a corner of the room is a desk and chair. On top of the desk is a *go* board and box of stones. Against the other wall is a standing wardrobe. I open the doors to find it full of clothes.

I look around again and realize the room and contents seem too serious, too grownup, for a teenage girl. There's no cute Hello Kitty stuff. No posters of boy bands. No stuffed toy animals.

Deciding to go all the way, I open the drawer underneath the desk. Inside, I find two file folders. I take them out and put them on the desk next to the *go* board. Both folders are tied closed with a red string. I undo the knot to one and open it. Inside are newspaper reports, pages of handwritten notes, and other documents related to Noriyo's disappearance. I open the other folder—it contains pages of poetry. I recognize the professor's handwriting.

Going back through the first folder, I glance through the contents until I stop at a timeline of her last few days: her school schedule, whom she talked to, what she said. The timeline indicates she never came home from the Saturday morning session at school. Along with the other notes are some police reports on possible sightings, more interviews with acquaintances, teachers, and others. I'm surprised to see all the reports from the police. It seems unusual that he would have them. I assume that the police don't let those kind of things out of their hands.

I find a police transcript of an interview with the professor. They asked him about Noriyo's mood, his relationship with her, and his whereabouts the day she went missing. He answered that she was in a good mood in the days before her disappearance, although he hadn't seen her too much as he was busy at the university. He claimed his relationship with her was typical of a father-daughter, not overly close but respectful. He claimed to have no knowledge of anyone who might have kidnapped her. And he knew of no reason why she might have run away.

Noriyo's mother gave a more vague answer about her relationship with her daughter, saying that it was "fine, except for communication." She stated she didn't believe her daughter would run away.

There are two other interviews I find interesting. One is with Tetsuo Iwaki, the *go* coach at Noriyo's middle school. He told the police that he hadn't seen her since she'd been in middle school. It's almost word-for-word what he told me six years later. The other is an interview with Mariko Okayama, the friend I couldn't find. In the interview, Mariko mentioned that she thought Noriyo had given up on the high school *go* team because she didn't like the coach.

I skim back through the files, find and study the timeline. I see that Noriyo was supposed to be in *go* club three days before she went missing. Looking back at the middle school coach's interview, his alibi for the day Noriyo went missing was that he was at a *go* tournament in Tokyo.

The last thing in the folder is a stack of New Year's cards from Noriyo's mother. I glance through them, each with the short line about Noriyo still missing. I add the return address to my notes then return the folder to the desk.

I go into the kitchen with the folder of poetry and put it on the table. In the refrigerator I find some eggs and fruit. I make a quick omelet and fruit salad. While I eat, I look at the contents of the other folder. There is one poem per page. A date on each page shows that the poems are in chronological order. The first is about six months after Noriyo went missing, the last two weeks ago. The content of the poems varies, from direct laments about his daughter's disappearance, to more indirect references: silence, shadows, thoughts.

One poem talks about the pain he must have caused her, that he will set it right if he can. If only he knew what he did, if only she'd return to tell him what he did.

Language evolves partially through metaphors.
When we say we are "up" (meaning "happy")
it is largely derived from metaphors for "up
is good" and "down is bad." That we have
the cognitive capacity for metaphor is easily
explained by our brain's neural makeup: It's a
lot easier to understand something in terms
of what we already know than to develop
completely new neural patterns. That way we
don't have to come to every situation having
to exactly match our previous knowledge. In
essence, our brains are metaphor-making
machines. As we make our way through the
world, we are constantly trying to match what
we experience with what we have already
experienced, and if we encounter something
new, we try first to match it with something
we already know. An efficient, if not always
accurate process.

Literature and art are essentially a highly
refined expression of that mental functionality.
The concept of *mono no aware* applies as
a literary theory, or at least the ideal of all
literature, and as a way of theorizing about how
readers understand what they read. Emotion
and metaphor are keys to both.

40.

TAKING CHEAP LOCAL TRAINS, it's night when I arrive in Tokyo at Harajuku Station. Before I left Numazu, I called the professor and asked if I could leave my stuff at his house for a couple of days. I tell him I'm going to check out a job possibility in Tokyo. He said I could leave my things as long as I needed.

I feel drawn to Tokyo by circumstances more than for any logical reason. First there's Junko Miyake, the performance artist and suicide victim. I want to find out something, anything, about her reason for committing suicide. It's a task unfinished and I'm curious. Second, Noriyo Imai is possibly in Tokyo. True, I reached that conclusion without much evidence. Well, no evidence other than the fact that she ran away to Tokyo before. But Tokyo is a big place with a lot of people and if I were going to disappear, this is where I would go.

I'm also here to get away from the professor's house. It was too, I don't know … intimate. Yes, that's it. Intimate. I felt too intimate with the professor, not sexually of course, but intimate with the trappings of his life. There was too much of him there. I spent so much time with him over the past months, yet I knew so little about him. I developed an image of him as scientist, as poet and literary theorist, as whiskey drinker. Now, in a short time, I've learned about his personal life and it's nothing like I would have guessed. I'm not sure why that makes me feel uncomfortable but it does. I need the anonymity, the personal distance, you find in Tokyo even when you are crammed against half a dozen bodies in a subway car.

The streets and sidewalks are relatively empty tonight. It's in the middle of the week and a light mist is falling. I walk toward Yoyogi Park without having to dodge too many people. As I near the edge of the park, I see only three performance art groups doing their thing this night. Luckily one of them is the suicide foursome. They are in the middle of their play.

Only a handful of audience members watch the performance. Miki is not one of them. The mist is still falling, the water collecting on their heads and dribbling down their faces and shoulders. The four are dressed identically in jeans and white T-shirts.

I have to wait for twelve minutes for them to finish. They come back to life so suddenly that I'm startled. As they wrap up for the night, I walk up to one of the performers, the one I previously asked about Junko Miyake.

"Excuse me," I say and show him the picture Kumiko found for me. "Do you recognize her?"

He takes the photo and holds it up to the gloomy amber of a streetlight. As soon as he looks at it, he says, "She's the Pink Doughnut Girl."

*

THE SUICIDE PERFORMERS AND I go to an open-late coffee shop. The performer who does all the talking is named Driver. It's a performance name, of course—he sits in the driver's seat of their imaginary car. Driver is twenty-seven and works as a freelance website designer mainly for artists and music groups. "No one famous," he said. "Yet."

Driver is telling me what he knows about Junko "Pink Doughnut Girl" Miyake. "I caught her act four, maybe five, times. She wore elaborate outfits. Always a lot of pink. Her act was mainly dance with spoken word."

"You mean poetry?" I ask.

"More like rap. Her topics were usually about women's rights. Abuse and assault, inequities in the workplace, groping on the trains. She had an edge of humor though that made it less pedantic than it sounds. Like, she raps about stuffing a fake penis in her underwear when she used to ride on packed, rush-hour trains. The gropers would get a huge surprise. Some of them would scream in horror."

We laugh at that.

"For her finale, she wore this inflatable beach or pool ring, also pink, with little bits of color glued onto it. You know, like sugar sprinkles."

I nod, get a craving for doughnuts again.

"She could do this amazing contortionist thing. Crawling in and out of the doughnut without using her hands. It's hard to describe." He grabs a napkin and finds a pen. He sketches a few of the moves she made.

The quick sketches do show her in unnatural positions, which are also sensual in the way good dancers can display their bodies. "What did the finale of her act signify?" I ask Driver.

"Beats me. I never asked her. I never talked to her actually. Anyway it's kind of an insult to ask a performance artist to explain their work."

"Did you know that she committed suicide?"

"No. Funny thing though, the last time I saw her was in the back of the crowd watching our show."

We get coffee refills and some doughnuts in honor of Junko Miyake. "I'm sorry to insult your artistic integrity," I say to Driver, "but why do you do your suicide performance art?"

"Why do you think?" he says.

"I've been thinking but I'm not sure. Maybe just to get others to think about what it means to die? Or maybe to show how to do it? Or to help convince people not to kill themselves by showing the finality of it?"

Driver shrugs. "I suppose each of us does it for a different reason. Maybe it's to keep us, the four of us, from actually doing it."

"What about these suicide clubs?" I take out the printout of the website information for the club Junko Miyake joined.

Driver says. "I know about them. Sometimes I go to them to see what the members talk about. You know, research for our act. Obviously I haven't gone through with it."

"What do they talk about?"

"It's funny. No one mentions why they wanted to do it, only how they were going to do it."

"I guess they've made up their minds. There's no turning back."

Driver nods and takes a bite out of his doughnut, pink with sprinkles.

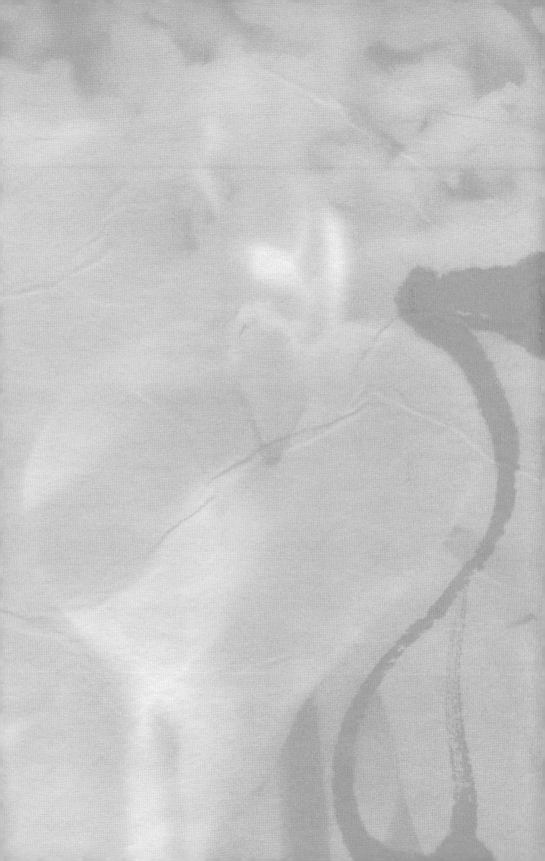

41.

AFTER A LATE BREAKFAST at the too-expensive hotel I managed to find late last night, I make the cross-town trip to meet Sumiko Imai, the professor's ex-wife. I called her as soon as I woke up and asked to meet with her concerning Noriyo. She told me her ex-husband called her about me.

I hadn't told the professor I was going to contact her. Sometimes it's like he can read my mind. I wonder what he told her. Probably warned her about an unstable American asking personal questions.

Riding on the subway, I wonder what I'm going to ask her. My explanation as to why I'm researching people who have disappeared or committed suicide sounds increasingly thin. My motives are vague even to myself, yet I can't change the direction of my inertia.

I'm also feeling desperate. I'm worse off than when I started. At least in L.A. there was structure to my unemotional life. Now I'm a puppet and events are cutting off my strings, my movements uncontrolled spasms.

On the other hand, it's as if I'm tantalizingly close to some kind of answer. And maybe the answer is Noriyo. Only she can tell me why she ran away. Only she can explain why she went to such an extreme measure, one which utterly changed the life of her parents. Her father changed from a focused, married scientist to a tragic poet.

Well, at least it's something to do.

*

IN THE POSH NEIGHBORHOOD of Hiroo, Sumiko Imai's address is a high-rise condominium complex. I'm wearing my best white shirt and dress slacks, which I ironed in my hotel room, taking advantage of the amenities. Even in my best clothes, I feel out of place inside the modern, expansive lobby.

I tell the receptionist whom I'm looking for and she calls her. I'm told to wait. I take a seat in an elegant but uncomfortable chair.

After several minutes, Sumiko Imai comes down. She's dressed in a stylish suit. Her hair is sculptured in an asymmetrical cut. She looks younger than her age, which must be over fifty. After we introduce each other, we sit in plush chairs in a quiet corner of the lobby.

I thank her for agreeing to meet me. "I'm sure it sounded like a strange request."

She looks at me with a blank expression. "So why are you interested in my daughter?"

"It's a long story. In essence, I'm doing some research and editing for the professor. I've gotten to know him fairly well over the last few months, at least on a professional level. Then I found out, somewhat accidentally, about his daughter ... your daughter's disappearance. The story is very tragic and I'm trying to understand it, both for personal reasons and for understanding some of the professor's work. I hope that make sense."

"In a vague way," she says. "What specifically did you want to know?"

"I have many questions but primarily I wonder if you have an idea of why Noriyo disappeared?"

"Assuming she ran way, and that's what all of us have come to believe, I have a very good idea of why she ran away. But I'm not sure I should be telling you."

"No, I suppose you shouldn't. I'm a perfect stranger," I say. "But what if I were to say I might be able to find her if I knew why she ran away?"

Her eyebrows raise. I'm not sure why I said that. I have no idea if I can find her.

"That's different," she says. "All right, you want to know why she left. Her father is a very rigid man. He demands a level of unachievable perfection. He broke her spirit. He chased her away." She gazes at me for a

258

long moment. "Feel free to pass that along to him."

Her statement intrigues me. I half believe it and half not. "I have to admit I don't know the professor very well, at least not on a personal level. But from what I do know, I have a hard time believing he would chase away his own daughter."

"You are correct about not knowing him very well. If you did, you would not find it hard to believe."

"Can you explain it to me?"

She sighs. "It's no secret my husband is a perfectionist, an unerring traditionalist, an ascetic minimalist, and believes only his opinion counts as fact. He controls all situations to his liking. He allows no humanity to exist in people around him."

A little wave of anger makes my face flush. "I agree he's a perfectionist and likes to control. But he's been very generous with me. Perhaps he's changed since Noriyo's disappearance?"

"I don't care if he adopted you as a son and gave you everything he owns. It does not change a thing about him." With that pronouncement she stands. "I really must leave. I do wish you luck finding my daughter. I would of course want to see her again. But she may not want to see me. And she absolutely will never see her father again."

*

THE HEADQUARTERS OF THE Kanto Go Association is not far from Hiroo. The building's interior is appointed with blonde wood and gray stone with black and white accents like a giant *go* board.

I'm asking the association's information technology manager to search their database for two people. One is Noriyo Imai, the other her *go* coach Tetsuo Iwaki. It took me nearly two hours to get this far. I had to explain the situation several times to several people before I wore them down and they agreed to help me. The "situation" I present to them is that I'm working for Noriyo's parents with a fresh lead we hope will reunite them with their daughter.

So far the IT manager found the coach participated in several officially sanctioned tournaments before and after Noriyo's disappearance. The records are detailed, astoundingly so. Unfortunately, my knowledge of *go* is pathetic so he has to explain each of the records to me. So far, he is being a patient fellow.

We zero in on the tournament around when Noriyo went missing. Iwaki placed fifth that tournament, one of his better results according to the records. The IT manager says, "He had a good run, beating a couple of solid opponents. He lost to the eventual winner but it was a close match."

That verifies he was in Tokyo when Noriyo went missing. "Does Noriyo Imai show up in the database? She is twenty-two years old now, sixteen at the time she went missing, if that makes a difference."

"She would play in the junior masters rank, ages eighteen to twenty-five." He enters the name and searches. "Nothing."

"How about Noriyo Iwaki?"

He gives me a questioning look, but tries that name.

"No."

"Can you search just Noriyo and just Imai?"

He does that. "Sixteen Noriyo and fifteen Imai."

"How about doing a cross-check for all players named Noriyo in the junior rank and who participated in the same tournament as Iwaki?"

It takes him a while to set up that search.

"Just one," he says. "Noriyo Okayama."

42.

OKAYAMA IS THE LAST name of Noriyo's friend I never found. Of course, I don't know if Noriyo Okayama is Noriyo Imai. But it seems likely— too many coincidences piling up otherwise. Honestly, I didn't have much confidence I'd find anything at the *go* association. It seemed like a real shot in the dark.

I had only my suspicions about the coach. He seemed to be holding back information, his knowledge obscured with pat answers. I can't say if he had an improper relationship with Noriyo. I didn't find any evidence of that. If he did, then he would be in serious trouble. If there is only a perception he did, he might still be in trouble.

On the other hand, Noriyo could have been pursuing him. It's entirely possible she developed a crush on him while in the middle-school *go* club. The coach might have been aware of her feelings if she couldn't restrain herself. Assuming he didn't feel the same about her, the coach would have only a few options: ignore her, dissuade her from pursuing him, or report her to her parents or school authorities. He wouldn't want to resort to the latter—the embarrassment of the situation would likely tarnish his credibility and standing at the school. I can imagine a scenario where he first tried to ignore her. When she continued her pursuit, he then tried to dissuade her. When that didn't work, he threatened to report her and she retaliated by running away.

Noriyo Okayama belongs to the Northwest Go Club, according to the information the IT manager printed for me. Along with her *go* records, the information includes her address and phone number. I try her phone number twice. Each time the connection goes immediately into voice mail. Rather than waiting to talk with her on the phone, I hop on the train that will get me closest to her address.

*

WHEN I ARRIVE AT the station, I find another faceless suburb, not that I'm expecting anything more. Like all suburbs they are built in a rush and only for convenience. Outside the station, I get oriented in front of a large map of the area. I find the street I'm looking for and head in that direction. It's not too far from the station, maybe a twenty-minute walk, so I don't have to spend money on a taxi.

If Noriyo Okayama is the professor's daughter, I want to talk with her without telling her my real reason. So I've concocted a cover story about researching *go* for an American magazine. I make a list of pertinent questions. It's easy to do since I know almost nothing about the game.

Noriyo Okayama lives in one of the ubiquitous three- or four-story suburban structures with businesses on the lower floors and apartments on the upper floors. I go up the stairs to the second floor. There are five apartments, hers is at the end of the walkway. On the nameplate "Noriyo Okayama" is written.

I listen at the door, don't hear anything from the inside so I push the buzzer. I can hear it buzz inside. There's no answer. I buzz again with no answer. I take out my cell phone and punch in her number while I listen at the door. I don't hear anything and her phone immediately goes into voice mail.

Not sure what to do, I lean against the wall for a while, then go and look over the open-air landing to the street. She might be gone for a few minutes or she might be gone for days, of course. If I only knew whether it is Noriyo Imai, then I would know if it was worth waiting for her.

I lean against the wall again for a few minutes. I go and ring the buzzer on another of the apartments on the floor. No answer. I try another, then another. Finally, a door opens a crack.

A young woman, with makeup half on, or half off, says, "Yes?"

"Sorry to bother you," I say. "I'm looking for Noriyo Okayama."

"Noriyo? She's in that apartment." She points down the walkway.

"Down there, huh? Thank you. By the way, is this her?" I show her the latest picture I have. "I've found three other women named Noriyo Okayama but they're not the right one."

She squints at the photo as if she needs glasses. "That's an old picture of her, but yes, that's her."

"Thank—" She shuts the door before I can finish.

After making sure there is only one entrance into the building, I go down to the street and find a place where I can watch for her. In a book store, I grab a book of poetry, pay for it, and sit on a bench provided conveniently for browsing customers. I figure the poetry won't distract me too much from my surveillance.

So far, I'm pretty happy with my sleuthing. Beginner's luck I suppose. It's surprising that the professor or his ex-wife didn't think about the connection with *go*, the coach, and Tokyo. Maybe it's because I don't have the emotional baggage of either of them to hinder my search. I'm operating with unbounded rationality. From my conversations with them about Noriyo, both were more intent on complaining about the other than looking for their daughter.

Actually I guess it's not true I have unbounded rationality. I'm tied to the professor in his dark world created when his daughter disappeared. I'm tied to it through my own search to understand and create my own emotional world. The two worlds spiral around each other.

*

I've been waiting in the bookstore for two hours. The clerk has been giving me the eye. I've read all the poems in the slim volume of modern poetry and started another. I've become skilled at reading with one eye and watching the building with the other.

I'm about to give up, at least make a move somewhere else, when I see a young woman turn into the building across the street. I get off the bench, nod to the clerk who gives me a relieved nod in return. I hurry across the street and into the stairwell.

She is walking up the stairs—I can hear her footsteps. I walk up as quietly as possible. When I get to the top of the stairs, I stop and slowly look around the corner. She enters Noriyo Okayama's apartment. Her shoulder-length hair hides her face as she leans forward to unlock the door.

When she is inside, I walk slowly to the door of Noriyo Okayama's apartment and put my ear to it. I punch in Noriyo's number. I hear a ring muffled through the door. I hurry away from the door.

"Hello?" she answers.

I swallow hard as I turn into the stairway. "Hello, Noriyo Okayama?"

She hesitates then says, "Yes?"

My hand between your legs,
has a mind of its own.
But then my mind has a hand of its own.
If the two could just get together
they might create ~~a symphony~~ the sadness
of pleasure.

43.

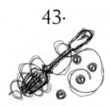

Noriyo Okayama/Imai agrees to meet me at a family-style restaurant on the same block as her apartment building. She bought my story of being a journalist interviewing *go* players, at least enough of it to meet me for a brief interview. "I'm not a very good player," she insisted several times. I explained—okay, lied—that the article is about everyday players, and I wanted to include the point-of-view of a young woman.

I'm waiting at the front of the restaurant when she comes in. She's changed both a lot and not much from the photo. Her face is nearly identical but her hair is shorter, less like a high school girl's. She stands like a confident, professional woman.

"Noriyo Okayama?" I say.

She gives me a little smile.

"Zack Hara," I say and reach out my hand like a good American reporter. She hesitates then she reaches out and we shake. "Thank you so much for meeting me."

"You're welcome," she says.

The hostess takes us to a booth. Sitting in it, I suddenly feel the family restaurant is appropriate. I feel like an older brother taking out a sister whom he hasn't seen for a while. "Perfect place for an interview," I say.

She looks around. "It's quiet enough."

I nod and look at the menu. "What do you recommend?"

"I usually get one of their pastas."

"Good idea."

When we've ordered, I pull out my pad of paper and pen.

"Which newspaper are you with?" she asks me.

"I'm a freelance reporter, working on, um, I don't know the Japanese word, but the English word is 'spec.'"

"Spec?"

"Short for 'speculation.' I write articles for potential publication, that is, without an agreement upfront. I hope the story on *go* will be published in the *Los Angeles Times*, but I'll be happy with any publication."

"I understand," she says. "What can I do for you?"

"There's more interest in *go* in the US. I'm trying to understand the Japanese perspective of the game from a regular, everyday player. So let's see, for the record, your name is Noriyo Okayama. And may I ask your age?"

"Twenty-two," she says.

"And your occupation?"

"I work for a small pharmaceutical company in their order fulfillment department. Our main product is a natural, over-the-counter sedative and sleeping aid."

"I could use some of that."

"You have trouble sleeping?"

"A little. Probably too much coffee."

"I'll be happy to send you a sample."

"Thanks," I say. "And you are single?"

"Yes."

"Are you from Tokyo originally?"

"Yes."

She answered that question without hesitation. "Enough of those questions. Thank you. How long have you played *go*?"

"Since I was in upper elementary school. It's been ten, eleven years."

"How did you get started?"

"In a school club."

"They have school *go* clubs? Please tell me what they are like."

"It was like any other school club. We met after classes. There was a coach who taught us how to play. The rules, strategies, etiquette. Then we would pair off for games, the short version when we first started, the full version when we got better."

"Did you play just in the club? Or were there tournaments?"

"Sure. In middle school and high school there were local, regional, national tournaments."

"How well did you do in them?"

"Not well at all. I didn't like tournaments."

"But you do now?"

"I still get nervous but I have more confidence." She smiles broadly and looks at me for a long moment.

"That's good," I say. "How often do you play now?"

"My club meets once a week, Tuesday evenings. There's usually a Sunday tournament."

Our pasta is served and we take a break from the interview. She is more relaxed and she asks me what other articles I'm working on. I hadn't thought of that, and I almost mention teen runaways. I quickly come up with a few: poetry, hot springs inns, performance art, suicide clubs.

She frowns at that. "Suicide clubs. Those are a bad image for Japan. What have you found out about them?"

"I've been following the case of four people who drove in a car to the edge of Aokigahara to commit suicide."

As I tell her the stories of the four victims, she is raptly attentive, our meals forgotten. It's as if she and I are the only two people in the restaurant, as if we are walking through desolate Aokigahara.

When first developed, the concept of *mono no aware* was not only a theory of literature but also a lens through which the Japanese viewed human nature. At the time, the dominant view considered desires and natural feelings as things to be controlled not expressed. This idea of self-cultivation was drawn primarily from Confucian and Buddhist beliefs imported from China.

44.

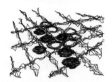

WHEN WE FINISH THE interview and our meal, I ask Noriyo, "I've never played *go*. I hope this isn't presumptuous but could you teach me? I mean just the basic rules and a general idea of the strategy. I would also like to take a picture of a *go* board and stones for the article."

She hesitates then says, "All right."

I pay the bill and we walk to her building and up the stairs. She lets me into her apartment with the disclaimer that it's small and she hasn't a chance to clean it lately. I tell her no apartment in the entire country is as small and dirty as mine. For the first time I hear her laugh.

To be correct, I should have said as small and dirty as my apartment *was*.

She turns on a light. The apartment is a studio with a tatami mat area wide enough to spread out a futon. There are two small windows, a horizontal slit in the kitchen above a tiny sink, and a vertical slit next to a bookcase holding a TV and boom box stereo. There are two doors, one to a closet and one to the bathroom.

She sets up a *go* board on a small, low table with nicked and chipped corners. We sit on opposite sides on purple-red cushions. We share a large bottle of beer while she gives me the basic rules and strategies of *go*. The rules are simple—alternate placing a stone on the board to surround and thus capture territory. The strategies quickly get complicated.

"Corner, side, center. Corner, side, center," she says in a mantra of the basic strategy of easiest to hardest kinds of territory to capture.

"Are you ready to start?" she says.

"I think so." I put down a white stone near one of the corners. "Corner, side, center," I chant.

She smiles and puts down a black stone. I'm not sure what to do next so I stall by asking a question. "It's a very meditative game, isn't it? Is playing your way of escaping?"

"Escaping? … I don't know if I've thought of the game in those terms before."

"We're all escaping something, aren't we?"

She points to a spot on the board and draws an imaginary line between our stones. "I'm escaping your attack with my defense."

I plunk down a stone, mostly at random, partly along the line she drew assuming she gave me a hint. "No, I mean, escaping the day-to-day pain of existence."

She plays her stone. "I don't think escaping those things are the way to live. Those things are part of living."

"Sure," I say. "But just to forget about them for a while … isn't that okay?"

"Making a change is the only way to eliminate them."

"It's not always that easy, is it?" I place a stone next to one of hers.

"It can be." She plunks a stone. "Is this kind of stuff going to be in your article?"

"I have a free-form style of writing. I'm looking for the essence of a story not the superficial aspects. I let the story take me where it wants to go, not the other way around."

"I'd suggest moving somewhere over here," she says, using her finger to draw a small circle.

"Okay." I pick a spot in that area and place a stone.

"Nice play," she says. "I suppose in a way it is escaping. When I do get immersed in a game nothing else seems to matter."

"Has it always been that way? Even when you were just starting, or maybe a little later when you had picked up the basics?"

She plunks a stone. "I'd guess that's true. It seems so long ago. By middle school I suppose."

"What about your coaches. What were they like?" I boldly ask.

"My coaches were good. They taught me well," she answers without hesitation.

"Good," I say. "Any particular one who was better?

This time she does hesitate a little. "Maybe my middle school coach. He is a good teacher and player."

"He wins tournaments, you mean?"

She places a stone with a click, slightly louder than usual. "He has won a few regional tournament, yes."

"I'd like to talk to him, if you don't mind. I like to get a coach's perspective."

She says, "He doesn't live in Tokyo and we don't keep in touch. Perhaps a coach from my club? Our head coach is a very dynamic *go* player."

"Of course. Thank you."

I play a stone. She plays a stone. I think she's winning. I ask her, "What about your parents? Do they play *go*?"

"No. They aren't interested."

"They aren't interested in the game, you mean?"

"Yes. That's what I mean."

*

AFTER WE PLAY FOR nearly an hour, she says, "I believe that's about all I can teach you in one sitting. I should get to sleep as I have to work early."

"Thank you very much. This has been very informative, very interesting."

"I hope you can write a good article."

"Eventually," I say. "I still have more research to do. In case I have more questions, may I call you again?"

"Oh," she says surprised, apparently not expecting that question. "Yes. You have my phone number."

"To be honest I've enjoyed our conversation in general. Not just about *go*. Do you mind if we might meet again soon?"

"Soon?"

"Maybe tomorrow?"

"The day after tomorrow?"

"Perfect," I say. As I turn to leave I notice a few things sitting on the book shelf I hadn't noticed before: a few books, a touristy mug full of pens, and a collection of five small stones each in the shape of an Asian pear.

Most of our experiences now come packaged, just as do most of our foods, designed to fit into our busy lifestyles. Digital media, package tours, theme parks, sterile subways, eliminate many of the opportunities to encounter *mono no aware*. The experiences they provide can be stimulating, of course, even moving by replicating real experiences, but rarely provide the individual, deeply affecting and quiet occasion of *mono no aware*.

45.

I MEET DRIVER LATE the following morning where he lives and works. He agreed to help me get inside of one of the suicide clubs. For my research, I told him. "Okay," he said. "As long as it's just research."

His place is in the back of an old house in the Yanaka neighborhood of Tokyo. The house belongs to his grandparents who live in the front. I bring my overnight bag with me. I can't afford to stay in the hotel and I hope Driver offers to let me sleep on his floor for a night or two.

His space is cluttered with computers, monitors, and other peripherals. Strands of tangled extension cords lead from the computers and power strips and, wisely, surge protectors. He clears off a stack of magazines from a chair for me.

"First thing," he tells me right off, "you need an alias."

"You mean a fake name?"

"That too but I mean an alias IP address, your computer's location. It's necessary so no one can trace you."

"Who would trace me?"

"Probably no one. But you don't want someone busting up the group by tracing you. It's against the law to plan group suicide. I'm trying to make it as safe as possible. For you and me."

It takes him only about five minutes to set up my alias and screen name—MABOY. I take a guess: "*Monono Aware* Boy?"

"Right. Let's log you in and see what's up." Driver takes us to a website and logs me in. A home page comes up. He points out the various features of the site: the disclaimers, suicide help resources, general information links, then the forums. Each of the forums is dedicated to one aspect of suicide, to those who tried it and failed, to those now determined to carry it out.

He goes into the "determined" forum. There he finds several listings for those searching for others to join a club. After further searching, he finds one looking for one more member. He looks at me and I nod.

Apparently the suicide club is in a hurry. My application is approved in ten minutes. I'm given directions and a time to meet with the rest of the group. When I asked in the chat window if I needed to bring anything the response was: "Like what?" I guess I thought they might want me to bring tape or charcoal or lighter fluid or something.

*

I'M WALKING FROM THE subway, following the directions on the map I was sent from the group. It's close to midnight. I'm not sure why they want to meet so late but I don't care about the time and likely neither do they. Maybe it's the only time their schedules would allow.

I stop and check the map. There are a couple of pachinko parlors on opposing corners. It reminds me of Pachinko Boy and his failed heist. I think I should get a tattoo. I wonder why I think I should get a tattoo. I walk ahead another block then stop trying to find the street where I'm supposed to turn right. I see it ahead one more block. I pass a pharmacy and wonder if that's where they, we, will get our sleeping pills. I pass a little hardware store and wonder if that's where we'll get our tape and charcoal grill.

The street isn't much more than a narrow alleyway. I turn right and pass three *izakaya*—little drinking and snack places—each with enough room for ten customers at most. Across from the third one is the building where the club meets.

I walk into a hallway and find the room number. I listen at the door, hear a muffled voice. I hesitate before knocking, feeling jumpy, more than nervous. If someone touches me on the shoulder from behind, I'll jump out of my shoes. I ring the bell. The door opens a crack. I'm immediately hit with the smell of cigarette smoke.

"Yes?" says a shadowy figure behind the door.

"I'm Maboy."

The door opens. "I'm Biwa," says a man in his late thirties or early forties with streaks of premature gray in his hair.

"Biwa? Like the lake?" Near Kyoto, Lake Biwa is the largest in Japan. He shrugs. "Whatever. Come in."

Standing behind Biwa are two other guys, both about Biwa's age, maybe a little younger. One introduces himself as "John Wayne," oddly so since he's a slim, short guy with glasses. The other is "Golf"—as in the car, he clarifies, not the game. He's a tall guy, taller than I am, not that I'm that tall.

We sit down at a table. I'm given a glass and beer is poured into it. My three new compatriots raise their glasses and give out a startling loud toast: "*Kanpai!*" We down our beer and the three light up cigarettes. When I'm offered one and decline, John Wayne says, "Smart. Smoking is bad for your health. John Wayne died from lung cancer, you know."

No one laughs at the absurdity of it so I don't either.

Biwa says, "The main rule we have is you must be serious about taking your life or what we call 'going all the way.' We aren't here to talk you out of it. We aren't here to talk you into it. We don't want to know why you want to go all the way. We don't want to hear your story because we are not therapists. If you decide to change your mind or have any hesitation, you must let us know immediately. We won't hold it against you. We're only here as a group to facilitate the ultimate act. We feel that doing this as a group provides a greater chance of success. Our sole purpose is to plan when and how."

Biwa stops there. John Wayne and Golf nod.

I nod too and say, "Understood."

Our brains discard much of our daily existence because most of the moments in which we exist lack significance. It's easy to go through the daily grind without processing much of the information that bombards us. We perceive just enough of our environment to get around without walking into walls or driving off the road. When we don't have any unique experiences, then that day is lost in the dust of countless days.

To flow peacefully yet attentively with life instead of fighting against it is at the heart of *mono no aware*. It is a fundamental principle behind Japanese arts, which are typically pursued as *dō* or "way"—judo, for example. *Dō* also implies learning a skill not only for its own sake but also as a way of life. The master archer who teaches *kyudō* ("the way of archery") to the Japanese Emperor's Imperial Palace guards says that learning *kyudō* is not intended to be used as a defense of the Emperor, but as a way of thinking, concentrating, learning to stand with good posture. It builds confidence and mental awareness. Hitting the target is merely a test to see if the practitioner is being true to what really matters.

46.

I'm waiting for Noriyo to get off work. Her company's offices and warehouse are a couple of subway stops from her apartment. Her company is in a semi-industrial area, neighbors with an electric and plumbing wholesaler, a soft drinks distributor, and buildings housing several small businesses. One of the small businesses, weirdly, is a charcoal distributor.

Nervously pacing in the front of Noriyo's company, I'm sure I look like a criminal casing the joint for a robbery. In addition to my nerves, I'm feeling unsettled after last night's meeting with the suicide club. As if we were a committee planning a company's picnic, we impassively debated alternative plans, from car asphyxiation at Aokigahara, to a group overdose of sleeping pills in Biwa's apartment, to a mass jump at Kegon Falls at Nikko. We didn't agree to anything yet as we were supposed to be brainstorming. We did agree to think about the plans before the next meeting, each coming up with a first and second choice. We also talked about the pros and cons of leaving a note, how to have one's will in order, other details like those. All in all, it was quite a display of democracy and efficiency.

I'm not sure why Noriyo wants to meet me at her company. She suggested it when I called about seeing her again. She asked if I wanted to continue the interview or if this would be a date. She is a very direct person, definitely a trait shared with her father. I said I was finished with the interview. "Good," she said.

Noriyo comes out of the building carrying a plastic bag. She says, "We're going to walk a little way to a special place I know about."

I offer to carry her bag and she lets me. "Did you practice *go?*" she asks. With a laugh, I say, "No, sorry. I haven't had time since we talked."

"Busy writing your article?"

"Doing more research," I answer.

"About *go?*"

"No, another story." I laugh again. "It's about *mono no aware.*"

She looks puzzled. "It has something to do with cherry blossoms?"

"That's the classic example. I've found that not many people have heard of *mono no aware*. I'm still trying to understand it myself. But it's about our emotional response to things and events. Being able to see, to feel, the true or deeper connection between them and our inner life. When we experience *mono no aware* we feel the need to express our feelings."

She thinks for a moment then says, "That's a good explanation. It's a natural part of being human."

"It should be, shouldn't it?"

We come to a very narrow passageway between two buildings. Noriyo says, "The place where we are going is down here a short way. I'm sorry it's a little difficult."

I hold the bag in front of me to negotiate the narrow passageway. When we get to the end there is a little gate. Past the gate is a garden about the size of a double-car garage. There are some bonsai pines, a little patch of grass, a pond made from stones, and a tiny wooden platform under a roof.

She brings us over to the wooden platform. "I was walking at lunch one day and saw the opening we just walked through. Something seemed to be drawing me inside. When I found this little garden it was full of trash, the plants barely alive. This seating platform was falling down. It was a place of incredible sadness, yet also happiness."

"Sadness because it had been abandoned?"

"Yes. And happiness because I could feel the presence of the person who built it, could feel how much of his or her life he spent here. Every time I work here I discover something new."

"You must have spent a lot of time fixing it up. How could you do it all?"

"Just a little bit everyday. Pick up a bag of trash. Trim the bonsai. Water the grass. Fix a loose board. It's not perfect, of course. The plants don't get much sun and I don't really have a green thumb."

"It looks like you do to me."

We look at her work for a while, then she asks, "Would you like some tea?"

"That would be nice."

"It will take a few minutes." She shows me an old brazier she found buried under debris and cleaned. From the plastic bag she takes out a small bag of charcoal.

*

AFTER THE CHARCOAL IS glowing, she sets an iron tea pot full of water above the coals. While we wait for the water to heat, she shows me around the garden, telling me about nearly every plant, every stone, every blade of grass.

When the water boils, she makes a pot of tea. She also brought some snacks.

I ask her, "Have you showed anyone else your garden?"

"You're the only one."

"Why me?"

She thinks about this. "It's because you seem like you would appreciate it."

"I wouldn't have thought myself the type. Why do you think so?"

"Hmm ... I can't put it into words. It's just a feeling."

She shows me some stones placed in the garden.

I pick up one. "I noticed that you had a collection of stones in your apartment. They had an interesting shape, rounded, like a fruit."

"A pear," she says with a nod. "Just a hobby of mine since I was little. I saw one and picked it up and showed it to my parents and said it was a pear. That made them laugh. Every year or so, I'd see another one. Just one of those strange things we do, I guess. How about you? Do you have any odd behaviors?"

"Me? I'm all odd behavior."

She laughs, refills our tea cups. She lights a candle she has stashed in a box near the platform. "It's getting dark," she says.

I ask her, "Have you ever been lost before?"

"Lost? I don't think so. Oh, when I was a little girl, I got lost in a department store. A clerk found me crying and they announced over the store intercom that they'd found me and asked my parents to pick me up. It was embarrassing. Why, have you been lost?"

"Recently, I got lost in the Aokigahara Forest."

"What were you doing there?"

"Just hiking. I know, a strange place to hike. How about committing a petty crime? Have you ever done something like that?"

"A petty crime? You ask very strange questions. Your free-form reporting style? This won't be in your story will it?"

"I'm just curious."

"Okay. At that same department store where I got lost, I slipped a little toy cat into my pocket. I remember taking it because it looked like a stray cat that hung around our house. The toy was orange and white just like the cat. When we got home my parents found the toy. I had to return it to the store and apologize. Is that a petty crime?"

I nod.

She says, "I think you have another motive for your interview. I don't know what it is yet."

"Let me know when you do."

*

WE LEAVE HER GARDEN when the candle goes out. As we walk back to the subway station to catch trains going opposite directions, I realize she sees *mono no aware* in everything. Just being near her, I feel drawn into her life, wanting to understand her deep emotions, to understand why she ran away. I want to know how she can feel so much *mono no aware* when I feel so little. But how can I ever understand her? Why is she living a quiet, dark life hiding from her father? Why did she fall in love with her middle-school *go* coach, who may or may not have rejected her advances? Why does she play *go* with such passion? What does she see in a tiny, abandoned garden?

Maybe I'll never understand. Maybe it's my immutable trait not to understand.

Watching the leaves fall
in late autumn,
they ~~lie peacefully~~ rest on the ground
some face up, some face down.

47.

I'M BACK IN NUMAZU and I walk past my old apartment. There's a light on in the window. A shadow of a person crosses it. I keep walking. My first stop is Mama-san's bar. She greets me with a friendly "Welcome." She sets me up with a beer and something to eat. She asks how I've been, her voice flattened with concern.

"I'm fine," I say. "How are you?"

She laughs. "No one asks me that. But I'm fine, thank you."

"That's all that matters."

"Your friend the professor was in earlier."

"How is he?"

She titters for some reason. "He's fine too. We're all fine, but not."

Of course she's right about that. "Where was he off to tonight?"

She looks away, through the walls. "You know. His club."

"The club," I repeat.

I wolf down some of the food and suck down a beer. Mama-san smiles at my appetite. While she replenishes my food and beer, I ask her, "Let's say, hypothetically, someone found out where the professor's daughter is living. Should the professor be told this information?"

Mama-san sucks in a breath. "You know where she is?"

"Hypothetically."

She starts to say something then stops. "At first I want to say, of course, he should be told. But I can see why this hypothetical person might want to keep the information from him. Noriyo must have had good reasons for running away. She could contact him if she wanted to but she's not ready. On the other hand, maybe the professor isn't ready to be told. He's working out why she ran away and until he understands maybe it's best to keep him away from her."

It's what I want to hear. I ask her for a pen and a piece of paper. I write down information about Noriyo's new life. Then I fold the paper several times, like an amateur's origami, and hand it to Mama-san. She tucks the paper into the folds of her obi.

*

THE PROFESSOR'S CAR ISN'T in the drive but the door to the house is unlocked. Inside, I take all my artwork, my poems, my books, the paraphernalia I've collected, and stack them into separate piles in a loosely meaningful order.

Then I get out of my clothes and into a robe. In the bathroom, I start the water to fill up the tub. I rinse off the travel grime then lower myself gingerly into the steaming hot water. When I'm in up to my neck, I take a breath and lower my head until I'm completely submerged.

Holding my breath, I'm thinking this feels pretty good, the hot water stewing my brain, simmering all the thoughts and memories together. I raise up, take a breath and relax against the side of the tub. And I think of …

*

I WAKE UP WHEN I hear the door to the bathroom close. The professor must have returned. I get out of the tub, dry off, and put on the robe.

The professor is in the sitting room, looking out onto the garden, a pot of tea on the table. I give him the little book of poetry I bought at the bookstore across from his daughter's apartment. "A souvenir," I say. "From Tokyo."

"Thank you very much," he says. "I shall read it soon. How was your trip? Successful?"

"Yes," I answer. "I found a job and will be leaving tomorrow."

"Congratulations." He pours me a cup of tea. "In editing?"

"For a pharmaceutical firm. Their main product is a natural, over-the-counter sedative and sleep aid." I tell him the name of Noriyo's company.

Without hesitation, the professor says, "I haven't heard of the company. Again, congratulations."

"I'll be sad to leave Numazu," I say.

"I will be sorry to see you go. Will you continue your search for *mono no aware?*"

"Yes. I don't know if I will ever get there, but you've helped me immensely."

"You've helped me as well. More than you know."

If we were to develop an artful way of living based on *mono no aware*, it would be *mono-no-aware-dō*, or the "way of experiencing the deep emotional significance of objects and events." Or more concisely, the "way of aesthetic perception." A guiding principle of *mono-no-aware-dō* would be to understand the significance of the object or event. In Japanese, this is called *mono no kokoro* ("the heart of the thing") and *koto no kokoro* ("the heart of the event"). To be aware of the heart of something means to be sensitive to *mono no aware*.

There are many examples of how this notion might be applied. Nobel laureate Barbara McClintock talks about developing a feel for the organism so profound that she felt she had become the genes inside the corn plants she studied. Einstein said that scientists never think in equations, but rather visualize the nature of the phenomenon. The writer Isabel Allende said her writing comes not from verbal formulations but from somewhere in her belly. Poet e. e. cummings said that the artist is not a person who describes but a person who feels. All of these examples of non-symbolic and nonverbal thought require an awareness of sensual and emotional feelings.

48.

BIWA IS TIGHT-LIPPED WHEN he meets me at Mishima station. I follow him to his car in the parking lot. John Wayne is in the front passenger seat, Golf in the back. They give me a nod when I get in the back with Golf.

We drive away from the station. Biwa stays at the speed limit, obeys all the traffic rules. The last thing we want is to get stopped by the police; we're nervous and look guilty of something. I give him directions to Takegawa, the town at the edge of Aokigahara Forest.

"Did you get everything?" Biwa asks me.

I pat the bag on my lap. Inside is a bottle of sleeping pills from Noriyo's company. The label promises a natural, smooth sleep.

"Everything else is in the trunk," John says.

We don't say anything until we get to Takegawa and I ask Biwa to stop at the convenience store. "I'm thirsty," I say.

We all go inside. The clerk who studies accents is working. He recognizes me. "Hey, Southern California. Still doing research?"

Biwa looks at me, eyes wide.

"No," I say. "Just out for a drive."

The clerk gives me a nod. "Enjoy it."

"Thanks."

When we pile back in the car, Biwa asks me, "So what's this research?"

"I told you I checked out the area a couple of times. He was working when I asked him about one of the suicides."

"He might call the police."

"Don't worry. He didn't suspect anything."

Biwa grunts. I give him directions to the farmer's road.

We come to the turnoff and I point it out. Biwa says, "That's not much of a road."

"That's why it's private," I say.

John Wayne rolls down his window and sticks his head out. "Watch for rocks or potholes," he says. "We don't want to get stuck or a flat tire."

Golf rolls down his window and watches from his side.

"Not too much farther," I say. "There's a little clearing ahead that's screened off with a bamboo grove. A nice stream runs through it."

We bounce through ruts and over rocks, driving past the fields of rice and other crops.

"Up there," I say and point to the left.

Biwa pulls the car to the left and into the clearing. "Here?"

We look around and Golf says, "Looks good to me." John Wayne agrees and Biwa turns off the engine.

It's late afternoon and the shadows of the forest and mountain stretch over us. We sit for a few moments. I drink some of my water. Biwa gets out, stands by the car and takes in a few deep breaths. John Wayne and Golf join him and take deep gulps of air as if they've never smelled a forest before. Apparently too much fresh air for them, the three light up cigarettes. I get out of the car and lean against it.

When they've finished smoking, Biwa reaches back in the car and flips the latch that opens the trunk. Like robots following a programmed script, we unload the hibachi and charcoal from the trunk.

Ever our leader, Biwa says, "Here's what we do. Get the charcoal going out here. We tape up most of the car, everything except one door. Then we take the sleeping pills, wait a few minutes for them to start working. Then we get in the car with the hibachi, then tape up the last door."

We all grunt in assent.

Golf pours charcoal in the hibachi. John Wayne sprinkles on the lighter fluid. Biwa lights a cigarette, takes a couple of drags, then drops it onto the coals. They burst into flame.

When the flames die down, we start taping the seams inside the car.

It goes quickly.

I hand out the sleeping pills. "Only three each," I tell them. "Or else you might throw them up."

John Wayne says, "I feel like throwing up already."

That makes me laugh. No one else laughs. We swallow our sleeping pills without ceremony.

*

WE GET IN AND Golf drags the hibachi inside and sets it on the floor. "It's kind of hot," he says with a lethargic voice. "I hope it doesn't start the car on fire."

I say, "Yeah, we wouldn't want to be burned to death." My leg is too close to the heat of the hibachi and I shift away.

Biwa says, "It will be okay. Just get the door sealed, quickly."

Golf slams the door while John Wayne tears strips of tape and seals the last door.

We are quiet for several moments before Biwa says. "Goodbye."

Golf says, "Goodbye."

With a quiver in his voice, John Wayne says, "Goodbye."

I say, "Goodbye."

That's all we say.

I look out onto the forest. It's getting dark now or it might be my consciousness growing dim. I'm feeling heavy, weighted down into the car seat. It's getting hot too. Sweat beads on my brow. I try to wipe it away with my sleeve, but my arm falls to my side.

Someone sniffles quietly. Then someone else. I hope it's not John Wayne—it wouldn't be good for his image.

I'm waiting for my life to flash in front of my eyes. I'm waiting for the last bit of my life and a sudden insight. A fullness of complete awareness. A death poem. *Mono no aware.*

So far, nothing. I relax, yawn.

*

MY MIND WANDERS OVER a flattened, featureless terrain. Where I hope to find deep, lucid memories I see only two-dimensional images. A photo of a truck. A manual on water tower design and field erection. A field of tree roots but no trees, the washed-out remains of a village, a whiskey bottle label, a slice of pear in the shape of a stone, a shimmering liquid garden, a tree clinging to a cliff, a wilted cherry blossom.

The professor recites a poem, something about a frog in a well. When he finishes, he laughs. Then Noriyo moves a *go* stone and laughs. Miki sucks on a straw stuck in a root beer float and laughs. Setsuko Yone hands me a newspaper article about my grandfather and laughs. Kumiko shows me a wilted cherry blossom and laughs. Johei reads a poem and laughs. The police detective slams the jail door shut and laughs. Mama-san tears up a piece of paper and laughs. Driver sits up in his fake car and laughs. Carine holds a set of keys out of my reach and laughs. Joe laughs just to laugh. The bastard.

*

I OPEN MY EYES to find it's pitch black inside the car. But my eyes are still clamped shut. I force one eyelid open a mere slit. A streak of light pierces my brain and the slit closes. I'm in darkness again—a shadowy world of people, things, images.

When I was a little kid, I once dreamed I was drowning. Going under for the last time I discovered I could breathe underwater. I was happily swimming like a fish until I knew I wasn't a fish and that I really was drowning. That's how I feel now.

I know why. I've come close but failed. I should have found *mono no aware* in the blizzard of cherry blossoms when Kumiko took my hand at the beginning of our relationship which turned out to be as ephemeral as the blossoms. Or in Johei's poems, his "big ambitions," which mean everything to him, nothing to anyone else, and their worth will die with him. Or in Noriyo's secret garden where she found joy. Or in the simple life of the convenience store clerk who can detect hundreds of accents. Or in a pear-shaped rock, in the sound of polished stones tumbling in the surf, in the caress of water in a hot springs bath.

Most of all, I should have found it in the professor's search for *mono no aware*. I realize now that he was struggling to grasp the concept through his research, in his poetry. For without *mono no aware*, he will never understand why Noriyo left and without that knowledge he will exist in constant pain. It's why he assigned me the tasks taken from his daughter's life. He wanted me to experience them, to understand them, to explain them to him. Bringing *mono no aware* to him was my ultimate, fundamental task.

But if I can understand such emotional depth in another person, I must have found some emotional life inside me. Yes! It's there, maybe always was, hidden deeply. Something, someone pried it out into the open.

But it's my last lucid thought—beautiful in its transparency. Before it's gone in a flash, I want to tell Biwa and John Wayne and Golf. I try to move my hand to touch them, wake them up, tell them.

I'm flooded with love and loss, joy and sadness, delight and disgust. Pure emotions without beginning, without end, without context. I want to shout about their power, wallow in their fullness.

*

THICK BILE RISES UP to my throat. I try to swallow but it sticks. I gasp for breath.

With super-human effort, I slide my hand toward the door handle. At last my fingers touch hot metal. I try to lift the handle but I have no strength. I want to pull it, throw myself against the door, fall to the ground, smell the earth. But I have expended all my energy.

My grandfather appears outside the car, shaking a shovel at me, yelling something, pointing to my shoulder, no, pointing to the door lock. I can't hear what he's saying. My arms are dead weights. My head falls back. I can't breathe.

He disappears. A shovel flies into the gl—

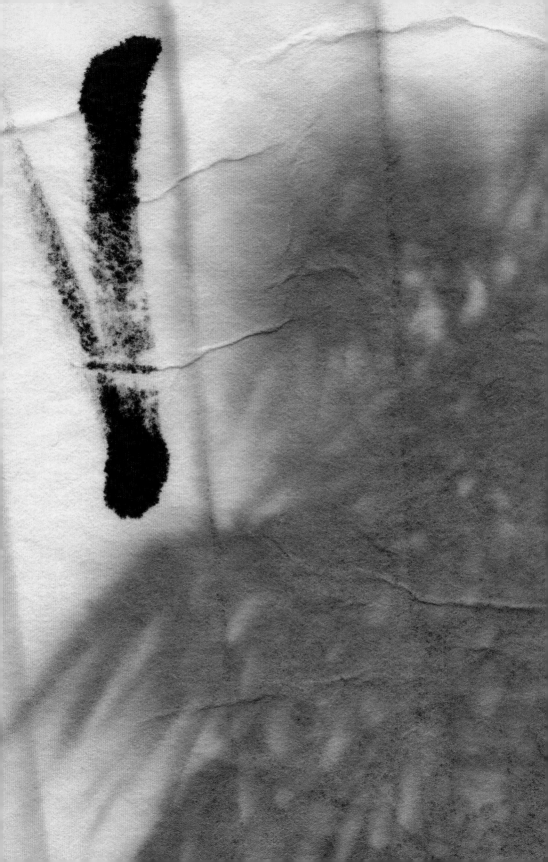

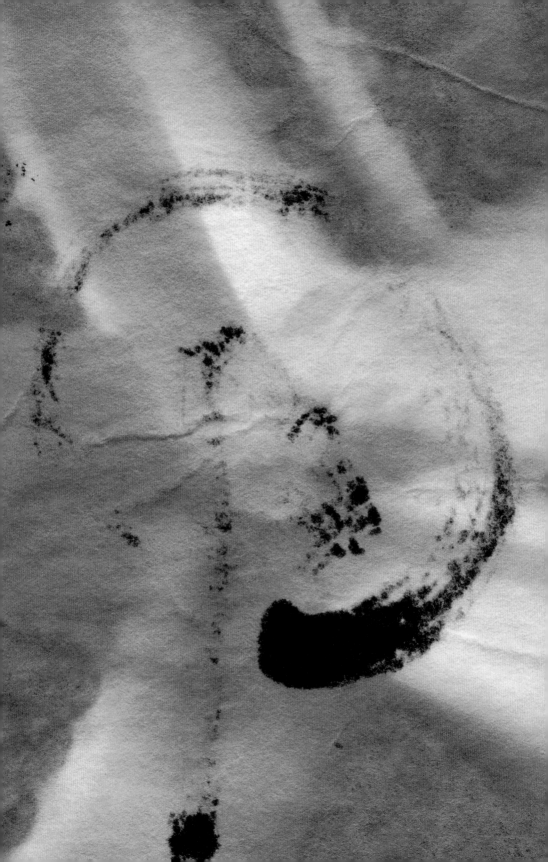

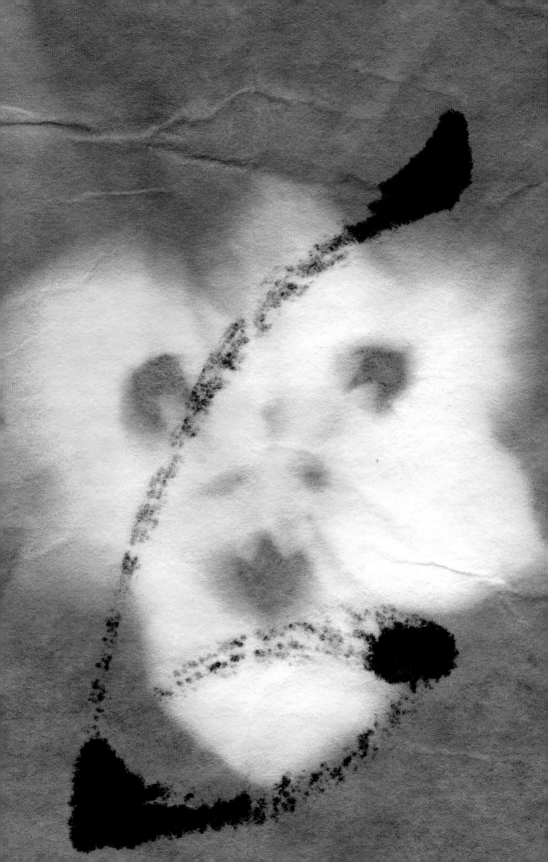

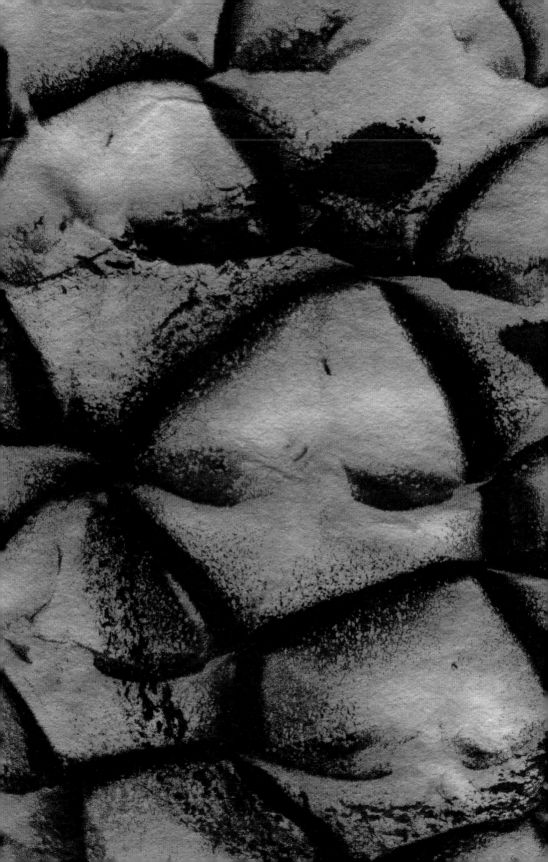

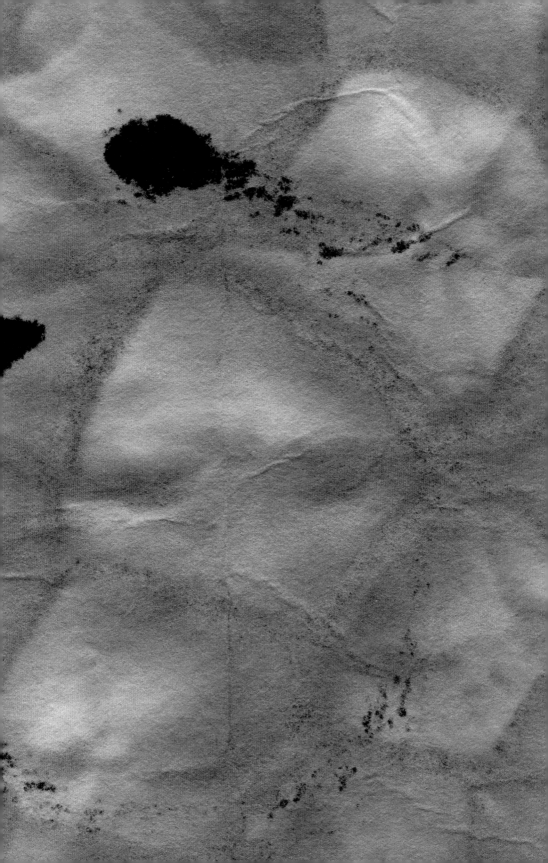

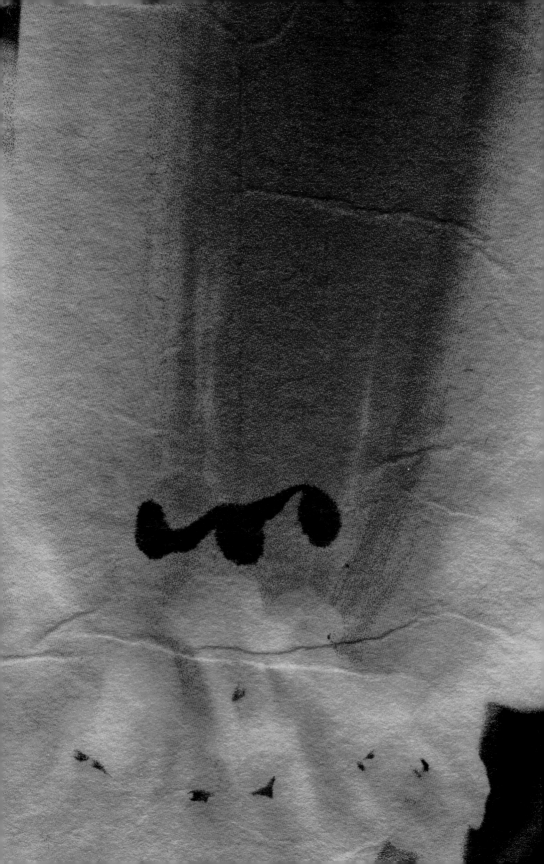

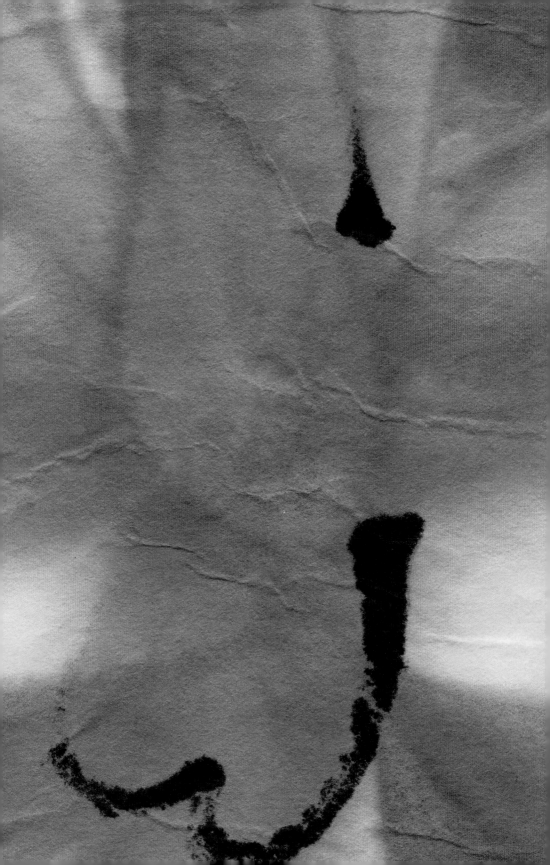

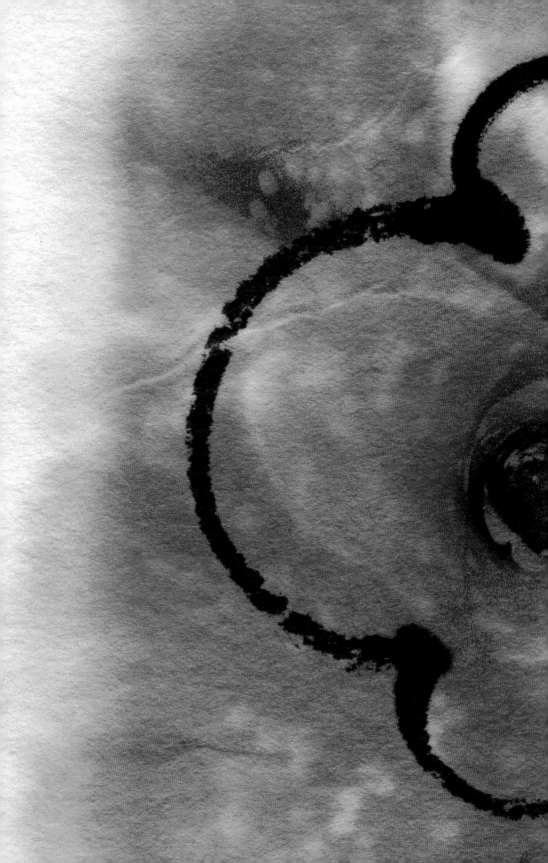

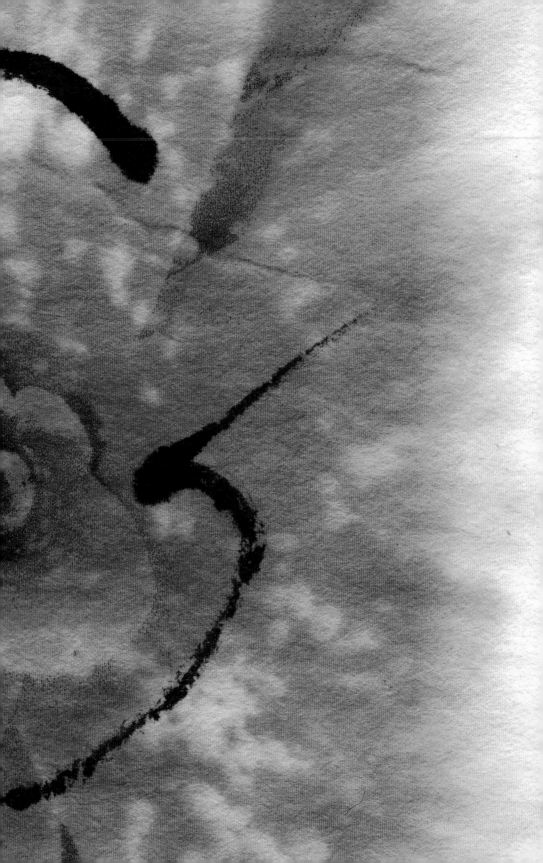

EPILOGUE

PROFESSOR IMAI FINDS THE stacks of art and sketches, poems and writings, and books. A box containing the pear-shaped rock, a whiskey bottle label, maps, and photos. He sits on the tatami and looks through the art and the sketches. He skims through Zack's writings about *mono no aware*, his poems and notes on suicide.

When he finishes, the professor knows what they mean—Zack believes he will never understand *mono no aware*. The frustration shows in his writing, in his images. His search has grown increasingly desperate.

The professor knows what Zack is going to do, why he left behind his things, the evidence of his search for *mono no aware*. He calls the same detective he'd called weeks ago when he turned in Zack for stealing from the bar and overstaying his visa. The detective answers and the professor explains he believes Zack and three others are going to commit suicide in Aokigahara. The detective says he will follow up on it and call him back.

While he waits, the professor begins to categorize Zack's things, placing them in organized piles. One pile is for "nature," one for "literature," one for "art," one for "relationships." A research paper is already forming in his mind: "Descent Into Sanity? A Case Study on the Effects of *Mono No Aware*."

The detective calls and tells the professor the Takegawa police discovered an attempted suicide of four men in a car near Aokigahara. The police were alerted by one of the local farmers who is a member of an unofficial civic group formed to patrol the area to dissuade would-be suicide victims. The detective says the farmer intervened, breaking into the car with his shovel. The four men were taken to the hospital in critical condition but expected to survive.

"Oh!" says the professor.

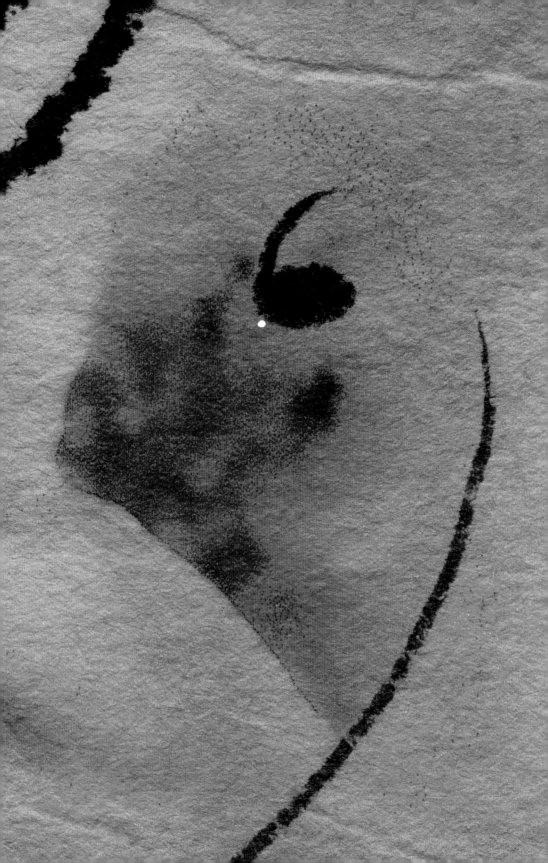

CHAPTER NOTES

CHAPTER 1

Gauloises, a French cigarette, has not been sold in the USA since 2004; how Joe got his is unknown.

The suicide website advertisement is a fictional translation based on a true story.

CHAPTER 2

Numazu (2008 population 209,000) and Mishima (2008 population 112,500) are real cities in Shizuoka prefecture. The Aokigahara Forest is also a real place. Other than Tokyo and other major cities, the towns and villages in the novel are fictitious.

The story of two lovers committing suicide in Aokigahara is from the novel *Kuroi Jukai* (Black Forest) by Seicho Matsumoto. Aokigahara, also known as the Sea of Trees (*Jukai*), is described as the "perfect place to die" in Wataru Tsurumui's bestselling *The Complete Manual of Suicide*.

CHAPTER 3

The poems are from these sources respectively:
- From *Shūishū*, Book IX, #511. Adapted from a translation by Mark Frederick Meli, *The Genesis of Aware: Emotion, Perception, and Aesthetic Value in Early Japanese Poetry*, Ph.D. dissertation, University at Buffalo (SUNY), 1997 p. 76.
- From *Kokinshū*, Book IV, #244. Adapted from translation by Mark Frederick Meli, p. 74.
- Adapted from Liza Dalby, *The Tale of Murasaki*, Nan A. Talese/Doubleday, 2000, p. 207.

Exhibit W006 sources are respectively:
- From a review of the movie *Ugetsu Monogatari* ("Tales of Moonlight and Rain")
- Howard Rheingold, *They Have a Word for It: A Lighthearted Lexicon of Untranslatable Words & Phrases* (Sarabande Books, 2000)
- http://haiku.ru/frog/glossary-engl/enggl.html
- Richard Hooker http://www.wsu.edu/~dee/GLOSSARY/MONO.HTM

- http://cla.calpoly.edu/~bmori/syll/Hum310japan/H310JapanVocab.html
- http://www.japan-zone.com/culture/literature.shtml
- http://www.michionline.org/resources/Glossary/M/mono_no_aware.html
- Rebecca D. Larson
- Yasunari Kawabata's Nobel Lecture, December 12, 1968
- Marie-Lise Assier

CHAPTER 5

The discussion of the current status of *mono no aware* is based partially on an informal survey conducted by Professor Takahisa Furuta of Gunma University, Japan. Professor Furuta asked colleagues and students if they ever used or heard the term *mono no aware*. No one could recall using or hearing it, and he concluded that modern Japanese do not use the term explicitly in daily conversations any longer. His understanding of the concept, at least its original meaning, is the feeling you have when something calmly sinks into your mind.

Today, the concept seems to have changed to mean "wretched," although Japanese, even under age twenty, have *mono no aware* feelings when they see something collapse into ruin. To the professor, modern Japanese have forgotten the spirit of *mono no aware*. One possibility for the change, he hypothesizes, is that the modern Japanese need a strong stimulus to be moved: their minds are blunter, or more dull, than they used to be one thousand years ago in the Heian period. Japanese are inundated with media, perhaps even more so than in North America.

Modern Japanese may just be too busy to appreciate the concept. Young people in Japan are dwindling not only in number but also in spirit, and few become interested in the time-intensive traditional arts or aesthetics. Also, the Japanese haven't fully recovered from economic recession yet [early in the twenty-first century]. The average Japanese has become very used to negative news and being disappointed in the last ten years and longer. Their hopes have been dashed for so long. The salary workers who are in debt with large housing loans and education expenses, remnants from the bubble economy of the 1980s, who are now getting laid off, seem particularly representative of modern *mono no aware*.

Now, Professor Furuta believes, most Japanese want to experience *yutori*, or calmness, a bit of leisure, in their lives. When they have recovered *yutori*, maybe then they can appreciate *mono no aware* again.

Re Exhibit W014: An example of a Zen *kōan* is "You never step in the same river twice." Or: The monks of a dying Zen master had all gathered by his bed, from the most senior to the most novice monk. The senior monk leaned over to ask the master if he had any final words of advice for his monks. The old master slowly opened his eyes and in a weak voice whispered, "Tell them Truth is like a river." The senior monk passed this bit of wisdom in turn to the monk next to him, and it circulated around the room. When the words reached the youngest monk he asked, "What does he mean 'Truth is like a river?'" The question was passed back around the room to the senior monk who leaned over the bed and asked, "Master, what do you mean, 'Truth is like a river?'" Slowly the master opened his eyes and in a weak voice whispered, "Okay, Truth is not like a river."

CHAPTER 6

Cognitive scientists study how our minds arise out of the "wetware" of the brain and body; how we think, act and, increasingly, how we feel. In short, cognitive science studies human nature. Cognitive science, formally named as such about fifty years ago, is a blend of the more established disciplines of psychology, neuroscience, computer science, philosophy, linguistics, anthropology, among a few others. Much of the work of cognitive science is interdisciplinary, such as when a linguist and a computer scientist develop computer programs that can learn and understand natural language (though not very well, at least not yet). Indeed, much of the original work of cognitive science was done in computer science, as the dominant paradigm used the metaphor of "the mind is

like a computer." And, therefore, a computer could be like a mind. That line of research quickly hit a wall: the mind is much more complicated than a computer, at least with our current hardware and software. Professor Takahisa Furuta writes in an email: "As you say, *mono no aware* is difficult to convey, indeed. There is one thing I noticed in your e-mail. You wrote '*mono no aware* is similar to empathy, or sensitivity, especially to the inherent sadness of things.' If your stress is on 'sadness,' it might not be correct. *Aware* is strongly related to sadness in modern Japanese language, but it was not necessarily so in ancient Japanese, at least when the works Norinaga referred to were created. It was, at that period of time, rather a gentle indication of being emotionally moved. Therefore, part of the concept should include sadness, but not wholly. But taking ancient *aware* for sadness is not rare even among us."

Re Exhibit W015: Details from Shigeru Matsumoto, *Motoori Norinaga*, Harvard University Press, 1970, and Michael F. Marra, *The Poetics of Motoori Norinaga: A Hermeneutical Journey*, University of Hawai'i Press, 2007.

CHAPTER 12

In Japan the rate of suicide per 100,000 people is 36 for males, 14 for females. In the US the rates are 17 and 4. Russian rates are 70 and 12. From http://www.who.int/mental_health/prevention/suicide/suiciderates/en/
The homicide rate in the US is about 6 per 100,000, in Japan it is about 1. From http://en.wikipedia.org/wiki/List_of_countries_by_homicide_rate

CHAPTER 13

See the previously cited Michael F. Marra work for an English translation of Motoori Norinaga's *The Sedge Hat Diary*. Sedge is a type of hardy grass growing in wet or marshy areas. Norinaga's two-week journey to Yoshino to view cherry blossoms took place in 1772. Yoshino is still the premiere destination for *hanami* (cherry blossom viewing). Home to some thirty thousand trees, Yoshino is also a UNESCO World Heritage Site.

Re Exhibit W027: Poem adapted from a translation in Marra's work, page 39.

CHAPTER 14
Re Exhibit W016: For an extended discussion see: Isamu Kurita, *Setsugekka: Japanese Art and the Japanese View of Nature*

Beginning year of Japanese main historical periods:

Late 5th century Asuka
710 Nara (Man'yōshū compiled in this period)
794 Heian (The Tale of Genji written ~1010)
1185 Kamakura
1338 Muromachi-Momoyama
1603 Edō (Norinaga 1730 to 1801)
1868 Meiji
1912 Taishō
1927 Shōwa
1989 Heisei

CHAPTER 15
The Japanese martial art referred to is aikido, a purely defensive martial art.

CHAPTER 19
Haiku is usually interpreted to be three lines, the first in five syllables, the second in seven, the third in five. In Japanese, however, a haiku is usually a one line poem of seventeen syllables. Modern, free-form haiku eschew a prescribed number of syllables but not the brevity. Tanka (also called *waka*) are thirty-syllable poems typically evoking the emotion surrounding an event. In Japanese tanka are usually written in one line but usually are interpreted in five lines of 5-7-5-7-7 syllables.

CHAPTER 20
Re Exhibit 34: Quote from Shigeru Matsumoto, *Motoori Norinaga*, p. 47

CHAPTER 23
Re Exhibit W035: For an English translation of Norinaga's essay see Marra's book previously cited.

CHAPTER 26
Re Exhibit W060: Additional discussion on emotion can be found in Victor S. Johnston, *Why We Feel: The Science of Human*

Emotions, Perseus Books, 1999.

CHAPTER 27
The *New Yorker* story discussed is "Year's End" by Jhumpa Lahiri in the December 24 & 31, 2007 issue.

CHAPTER 29
The poetry how-to book is probably Ted Kooser's *The Poetry Repair Manual*, University of Nebraska Press, 2005.

CHAPTER 32
In his monograph on suicide, "The Savage God," the English poet and critic Al Alvarez, a failed suicide himself, wrote that suicide is "a closed world with its own irresistible logic. Once a man decides to take his life, he enters a shut-off, impregnable but wholly convincing world where every detail fits and each incidence reinforces his decision."

CHAPTER 38
Re Exhibit 088: Kanji derivation from Kenneth G. Henshall's *A Guide to Remembering Japanese Characters* published by Charles E. Tuttle Publishing Co., Inc., 1988.

CHAPTER 43
Re Exhibit W102: For further discussion of Shinto, see Thomas P. Kasulis's *Shinto: The Way Home*, published by University of Hawaii Press, 2004. According to Professor Kasulis, most Japanese would describe their relationship with Shinto not so much as a set of formalized beliefs but rather a set of cultural traditions.

CHAPTER 47
Re Exhibit W125: See Michele Root-Berstein and Robert Scott Root-Berstein, *Sparks of Genius: The Thirteen Thinking Tools of the World's Most Creative People*, Houghton Mifflin, 2000.

EPILOGUE
"Thoughts are the shadows of our feelings—always darker, emptier, simpler." Nietzsche: *The Gay (Merry) Science* (*Die fröhliche Wissenschaft*, 1882)

LIST *of* ARTWORK.
BY L.J.C. SHIMODA